UNDER THEIR WATCH

"The heart of this novel is its vignettes into the lives of children who have suffered abuse, neglect, and abandonment at the hands of a parent or paramour. It is a raw, realistic, and shocking tale of dysfunction both in the lives of many families and in the child welfare system as a whole. This descriptive, easy-to-read novel is highly recommended for a candid look into our nation's foster care system."

—**JEANNE TRUDEAU TATE**, board-certified
adoption and child welfare attorney

"*Under Their Watch* couples creativity with firsthand knowledge of the commitment, challenges, and judgment of case managers in the child welfare system. Case managers work closely with parents to provide education and support to improve their parenting skills and stability. But the safety of the child always comes first. The two sides of this critical decision sometimes are at odds and require Solomon-like wisdom. A child's and family's future depends on making the best one. *Under Their Watch* digs down into and exposes the wisdom exercised by case managers."

—**LIZ KENNEDY**, child and family advocate
and founder of the Child Abuse Council

"An enthralling novel from start to finish, with characters that open us to both the brokenness and beauty of humanity. Ketchey brings a wealth of talent and experience to this work that makes it all the stronger."

—**WILL WELLMAN**, essayist and poet

"Charlie Ketchey's stories about caseworkers, single moms, kids, judges, police, and others are compelling and powerful. We are given new insights into how hard it is to work in the foster care system, with its demanding cases, paperwork, and difficult decisions. He makes a strong case about the importance of an impactful caseworker, a fair judge, and a just system."

—SHEFF CROWDER, CEO of the Conn Memorial Foundation

"*Under Their Watch* is a compelling, well-told story. Its characters breathe life into three fictional cases that capture the suspense, risks, and trauma of making serious family and child safety decisions. It is a frightful reminder that often, evidence ambiguity puts children and families at risk. The story dramatically exposes conflicts between the state, case managers, courts, and families seeking to reach safe and permanent solutions. *Under Their Watch* could be a master class case study."

—BOB GILBERTSON, inductee of the YMCAs of the Southeast Hall of Fame

UNDER THEIR WATCH

A NOVEL

CHARLIE KETCHEY

RIVER GROVE
BOOKS

Published by River Grove Books
Austin, TX
www.rivergrovebooks.com

Distributed by River Grove Books

Design and composition by Greenleaf Book Group and Mimi Bark
Cover design by Greenleaf Book Group and Mimi Bark
Cover image used under license from ©Shutterstock.com/Thichaa;
©Shutterstock.com/maxpro

Publisher's Cataloging-in-Publication data is available.

Print ISBN: 978-1-63299-906-1

eBook ISBN: 978-1-63299-907-8

First Edition

To child caseworkers

CONTENTS

Contents

Chapter 1

REMOVAL AND CUSTODY

Cameron Springer felt the frustration of loss but gave no visible reaction when Judge Crowe announced her decision. It wasn't a first for Cameron. She'd had her fair share of losses, but in this instance, the loss involved the sting of rejection. And she was afraid of some impending injustice, of things to come. Cameron's youth didn't insulate her. She often wondered whether she'd be able to handle stress better when she was older. Usually confident, she took things in stride and approached each day with positive expectations, but the courtroom was not a venue of control. Neither was family disruption.

Earlier, seated in a straight-backed wooden chair, Cameron, as a witness, had sworn under oath to tell the truth. Attorney Chad Burt faced her directly, notes in hand, head tilted down, eyes up and looking straight at her.

"Cameron Springer, you understand you are under oath and must tell the truth?"

"Yes," she answered.

"Did Kids Care Inc. appoint you to look after the two-year-old boy Elijah Santeroa?"

"Yes, sir."

"You are his appointed caseworker, charged to look after his interests, with authority and power to leave him with his mother or remove him to foster care?"

"To look after and make recommendations," Cameron said.

"And you did look after him, you did make an investigation, and you exercised your best judgment as to Elijah's welfare, and in your case file you recommended Elijah remain with his mother, Ms. Alisha Santeroa, correct?"

"Yes, sir."

"Now, today, you walk into this courtroom and ask this court to keep Elijah in the care of the state of Florida, not in the care of his mother, after you changed your mind yesterday afternoon and called a sheriff's deputy to take Elijah into the state's shelter, right?"

"Yes, but not foster care, just temporary shelter."

"And you did that because you don't like Ms. Santeroa's boyfriend, a man you met only one time, yesterday afternoon, immediately before you called the deputy and took Elijah into the state's care."

Cameron looked at Judge Crowe. "I visited Elijah and his mother at their apartment. The boyfriend showed up and was drugged and aggressive—anyway, that's how he appeared to me—and he was pointing at me, throwing his hands around, not understandable."

"Correct," Mr. Burt interjected, "but now the question is whether Elijah should be kept from his mother, who you specifically found to be a good, caring mother, according to your notes in the case file. You based your judgment on the boyfriend's behavior, not Ms. Santeroa's behavior, correct?"

While Cameron appeared confident, on the inside she was a jittery state of nerves and uncertainty. She continued, "Yes, that's right, but not the whole story. I have my responsibilities. The boyfriend is a bad influence and dangerous in that home. That was and is my assessment. I've worked as a care manager for over three years. I know the dangers of inappropriate behavior within a home; this is not a theoretical exercise. And if, in some way, my judgment is mistaken, it is not mistaken to any significant degree."

Burt continued, "But the mother is capable, and you could ask the court to issue a temporary injunction against the boyfriend to prohibit his presence in the home—that is an option and not onerous to Elijah and his mother, isn't it?"

Judge Crowe tilted her head toward Cameron, peered over her reading glasses, and said, "Mr. Burt makes a good point. What do you say to that, Ms. Springer?"

"Judge," Cameron said, "what am I supposed to say? Everyone knows it's best for a child to be left with the parent, and you could enter a restraining order against the boyfriend. Does that work? Judge, honestly, with all due respect, I don't think so. In fact, I've seen it have exactly the opposite effect. It's dangerous."

Judge Crowe didn't respond immediately one way or the other. The courtroom sat silent. The creaky floorboards were mute. The musty air of the old room became noticeable, with a scent of apprehension. No one stirred. Judge Crowe read her notes, a pencil in one hand, the other hand resting on the long table. They sat at a conference table, not a raised dais; this was not a courtroom that allowed a judge to stare down at her subjects. Even so, all in the room sat at the judge's beck and call, silently waiting for her next move.

Judge Crowe lifted her head and looked over at Cameron. Finally, she laid her pencil down and addressed her.

"I hear your argument, and I appreciate you speaking up. You base your testimony on the one episode with this so-called boyfriend. There is no drug test in this case and no testimony about abuse of drugs, or for that matter any testimony of violence in the home. And the petitioner here is a mother who wants custody of her son, and as a mother she is in a good position to make her own assessment. The court cannot discount that."

Turning to an attorney for the state, Judge Crowe asked, "What does the state of Florida say?" The attorney for the state agreed with Mr. Burt, saying there was little evidence to support temporary custody of the state, that the home study previously done was sound, and that a restraining order against the boyfriend might help.

Judge Crowe looked down at her desk, raised her head, and said, "I've heard enough," cutting short any further testimony from Cameron.

Cameron kept silent. Her mood abruptly shifted; she felt defiant, even combative. Maybe she would take a few days to snoop around and come up with more to say at a later hearing.

The proceeding ended, and the court ordered Elijah out of temporary custody of the state and back into his mother's care. In a passing remark, the judge suggested that the mother avoid her boyfriend. The court also gave Ms. Santeroa more time to complete her case plan. A case plan was a typical protocol of the state's childcare program, designed to teach a mother how to be a mother—not a perfect mother, but a safe mother. That was the idea.

Before moving to the next case, Judge Crowe took a break. With that opening, Cameron shot out of the courtroom, searching for the attorney Chad Burt and his client Alisha Santeroa. Cameron had something to say.

She knew after court hearings that those involved often hung around and discussed what had happened. Participants would confer in an assembly room, a large, open space scattered with chairs. There was little to no formality to the space. It was simply a big place with plastic chairs and few, if any, tables. The floor was linoleum. Not one picture hung on the bland, off-white walls.

Participants waited there before hearings too. Bailiffs eventually called their cases, one by one. Each would receive individual attention before the court, though most likely in a short, distilled manner. Elijah's case was longer than most because of the appearance of Attorney Burt. Cameron knew that he occasionally volunteered for free legal work, which had happened in this case. She didn't consider that out of the ordinary, although it wasn't every day that an attorney showed up for a parent.

Alisha was subject to case management orders of the court. Cameron knew Alisha had consistently carried out the court's directives, to her credit. Nevertheless, Cameron wasn't about to forget the boyfriend, Juan Martinez.

Although stark in appearance, like the courtroom, the assembly room would be a natural place to conduct some follow-up. Cameron walked up to Alisha and Chad.

"Alisha, I've got to learn more about this Juan Martinez. I didn't know about him until the other day." Glancing at Chad, she continued, "I doubt you, as the attorney, did either. Are you sure this guy Martinez is okay? I'm concerned. I'm not telling you how to lead your life, but *really?*"

"You know I'm looking for a job, and my mother is with me," Alisha said. "Elijah goes with her most of the time, and I have neighbors. Juan's not bad stuff. He's nice. I know him, same neighborhood."

"This might seem like none of my business, but in truth, it is. Does Martinez work? What do you know about his background?"

Alisha rolled her eyes, straightened, threw back her shoulders, and stared into Cameron's eyes. "I don't know, and I'm not saying. I mean, he works. He says so, has money. I mean, some. Not around much. I think he works, not sure what. He says he gets part time on the docks. Maybe he goes to the temp pool every morning."

"What else?"

"Nothing else. Isn't that enough? Back off. I gotta go. My mother is downstairs with a car. I'll call you, if the world doesn't fall apart." Alisha rushed off, and Cameron followed at a distance.

Downstairs, Alisha's mother drove up to the curb, and Alisha hopped in. Cameron heard only one thing—Alisha saying, "We can pick up Elijah, thank God." Alisha's mother drove off as Cameron watched from the curb. Then she hustled back upstairs for other court hearings. It was going to be a long day.

Chapter 2

UNEXPECTED VISIT

"**P**oor little fella," Alisha's mother said when Alisha got in the car. "That caseworker had no business taking him yesterday. Busting up all sorts of families. Not thinking about the child but about herself. Last night another guy and woman were on the news, got arrested, beat up their kid. I didn't see any government caseworker there."

"I got lucky, Mom," Alisha said. "An attorney showed up for me. Crazy, I couldn't believe it. Put that caseworker Cameron in a hole."

"Yeah, you're special all right, a special case of you know what. How many times, you know what I say. You need to grow up and get smart. You got no money. Got me. Otherwise, Elijah would be in big trouble. Anyway, I'm not going to keep him for good—just on occasion. That's it. This wouldn't happen back home in Venezuela. Men and women work and take care of kids. That is the way."

"Please, Mom, a million times, a million times, please don't go there. You got your old ways. I had a child at fourteen, the old ways.

You know what I mean. No telling where that baby is now. Miss her, it hurts. You do too. Let's not go there. I'm tired." With that, they fell into silence.

They got to an office of Florida's Department of Children and Families—commonly called DCF—and picked up two-year-old Elijah. He'd slept on an air mattress overnight, and he'd been fed, bathed, and looked after by DCF staff or someone affiliated with them. DCF alone never picked up kids, and neither did its private childcare organization Kids Care, where Cameron worked—it was the sheriff's job to pick up children and transport them as directed. Elijah was no worse off for the overnight experience—maybe even a bit better with food, ice cream, and air-conditioning over the last eighteen hours.

After picking up Elijah, they drove to Alisha's mother's house for dinner. Elijah played in the mother's backyard while Alisha and her mother struggled through some conversation about events of the past. They both needed to let go of feelings for the sake of the evening, so they pushed through.

After dinner, they put Elijah to bed and watched TV. The sun had yet to set. It was a Monday evening in June of 2009. They watched *The Bachelorette*, which took the edge off the day in court and the digging up of old bones in the lives of the mother and her daughter, Alisha.

Alisha's mother was of a different culture and had certainly encouraged Alisha to become a young mother at fourteen. Alisha ended up under the supervision of DCF but continued to live with her mother. After she gave up her firstborn to adoption, she left her mother and was strung out on drugs for a few months. DCF had stepped in with supervision.

After the show, Alisha picked up a sleeping Elijah, and her mother drove them to Alisha's apartment in Suitcase City, a multicultural neighborhood in the north part of Tampa next to the University of

South Florida. A little later, Juan Martinez showed up with some beer and food. He'd had a hard day at the docks and was in the mood for some late-night TV. They stayed up talking.

Eventually, Alisha said, "Cameron, the caseworker, has a problem with you. Not sure where this is going."

"What's wrong with me?" Juan asked indignantly, raising his arms and hands in mock surrender. "Are you crazy? I've done nothing but help you out. What's really going on?"

"Don't blame me. I supported you. Said you were nice."

Dropping his head and leaning forward on the couch, Juan said anxiously, "This is too much. I'm easy to target. Yeah, I was mad at that woman Cameron or whatever the other night and let her know she was giving you a hard time. You bet I wasn't happy with her, whatever color or half-breed she is."

"She's not a half-breed. Don't talk like that."

"Whatever, she's both dark and light and wronged you the other night, giving you a hard time about me and making threats about Elijah. Didn't like it. No way."

"Well, it went fine today: had my own lawyer and got Elijah back, judge didn't buy her stuff. That's good."

"Don't ever say I laid a hand on you. That'd be the end of it. Be careful. I don't want to step in any bad stuff. I'm working and don't need any trouble. I got to be squeaky clean, you know that."

"Got it. Look, I know you're a good friend. Sorry."

Juan nodded. "Okay," he said. "But for now, I'm leaving. It's 11:00, and I'm going to the corner to hang with friends. I got paid today."

But the evening wasn't over for Alisha. She stayed awake for another hour. At midnight, she heard a shuffle outside the door and peered through the front window. *Damn*, she thought, *Striker*. "What are you doing here? I told you to stay away," she said.

"Ahh, baby, don't talk like that. It's early, how about I come in and say hello. I saw the Spaniard leave. You still befriending him?" Striker had sharp, green eyes that glowed against his dark skin and black hair cut short and tight to his scalp. He was dressed in his typical dirty jeans and T-shirt. At least he had shoes on, Alisha thought, such as they were.

"Don't get into this tonight. I'll call the police. I told you Juan and I are friends, nothing more. He's a good one. I need a good friend. Not like you. Now get the hell out of here. I don't need your trouble."

He left, sauntering down the stairs and disappearing out of her sight. Alisha watched him go, locked the door, and braced it shut with a chair.

Chapter 3

A MOTHER'S WAY

After Alisha and her mother drove off from the courthouse, Cameron walked back to the courtroom. Other cases remained for consideration by Judge Crowe that day, and Cameron was the case manager for most of them. She didn't expect fights. On the simple facts and without any second-guessing, these cases involved children obviously removed with good cause: drugs, physical violence, malnutrition, and so on. These would be simple to explain but hard to cure. She listened and participated as called for.

But she kept drifting back to the earlier hearing, feeling anxious. She often felt an ill-defined unease about court decisions, even when courts accepted her recommendations. At twenty-five, she had been on the job for three years, and by now she sensed that she had little to no control over the future of the children assigned to her. In the case of Elijah, she was scared for him and his mother, Alisha.

Cameron wasn't a quitter; she knew she'd stick with Elijah and Alisha and do what she could for them. And she knew that the uncertainty she often felt also helped keep her on guard. Judge Crowe was known for her rigorous thinking and wasn't likely to accept the gut feelings of a young caseworker. But Cameron didn't trust Alisha's friend, the young man she knew as Martinez. His verbal attack and erratic gestures were enough for her.

The remaining cases that day were routine. The courtroom was a makeshift state office conference room dressed in drab government style. The room was functional but small, crowded, intense, and stiff. The judge sat at the head of a large conference table between flags of the United States and the state of Florida, with a little room to swivel her cushioned chair from side to side. Others in attendance were crowded up against each other in simple wooden chairs at the conference table. This was not a typical courtroom with attorneys separated into two or more different tables on opposite sides. Cameron sat on one side of the table together with the attorney for the state. The courtroom had no high ceilings, no pictures of venerable old judges, no grandiose columns.

When she'd started this job, Cameron hoped that the surroundings of her day-to-day work would be exciting and that she'd save the world, or at least a little bit of it. She was energized. She'd grown up in northern New Jersey, across from New York City, with a mother who was a nurse and a father who was a finish carpenter. Constantly working to learn better techniques and skills, they were dedicated to work they enjoyed. Cameron grew up comfortable and secure. Like her parents, she looked forward to rewarding and valued work.

Nothing was transient in her life. She had a stable home and one family, with a brother and two sisters. She was smart and athletic. She went off to college on scholarships and student loans. Nothing fancy, in line with what people thought and expected of her. She had her fair share of personal troubles just like everyone else: parents who were good-natured but not perfect and some not-great dating experiences with guys in college. Her biggest emotional issue was her strong connection with her little sister, Rosie.

After college, Cameron had headed to Florida on a lark, like many of her classmates. The idea was to get away from the cold and snow and live the beach life. Most headed to Miami and Ft. Lauderdale. Not her. She and her best friend headed to the west coast of Florida, landing in Tampa. She had a bit of a rebellious streak—maybe more than just a bit. She liked adventure. She had had some pocket money left over after school, and her friend had been game, so off they went. With her bachelor of arts degree in sociology, Cameron had landed a job with Kids Care right away. With a few weeks of instruction on the child welfare system, she was certified. Within a month she was making appearances in court, looking over the welfare of eighteen youngsters in the throes of family disruption.

Cameron's encounter with Alisha's boyfriend, Juan Martinez, was not her sole concern about the case. Over the course of her case management, Cameron had learned a lengthy history from Alisha, Alisha's mother, and other caseworkers. The story was disturbing.

When Alisha was twelve years old, her mother had invited a young man to move into their house. Her mother was from a small village in South America. She came to America with her husband, but within a few years, he died. She worked hard, leaving early in the morning and getting home late, working in wealthy homes in South Tampa, making sure there were groceries, calling on neighbors to look after Alisha, and keeping her daughter outside the hands of the state.

The young man was eighteen years old. He worked, carried out his responsibilities, and abided by Alisha's mother's expectations. She was grateful he was Hispanic. Those expectations expanded when Alisha turned fourteen and became pregnant by him with a baby girl. The young man was arrested for breaking and entering before the baby's birth, went to jail, and in a few weeks was out of jail and out of town. So the baby was born fatherless. Alisha and her mother put the baby up for adoption. All of this occurred before Elijah.

Cameron was convinced that this history had acted like some type of cancer within the bond of mother and daughter. Their relationship was strong but challenged. Alisha graduated from high school and got a job as a cashier with a large grocery store, but she had a hard time keeping steadily employed. She moved from job to job. When she was twenty-two years old, she met another boyfriend and had Elijah. There was no adoption this time. Alisha and her mother were both devoted to the boy.

When Cameron first read this story in the case file, she was taken aback. She tried to take the story in stride, to be worldly and open to different cultures. At the same time, she wanted to stay in line with how she thought of herself: a young woman supported by ideals, with a sensitivity to realities but steely in her own commitments.

When assigned to Alisha and Elijah, Cameron struggled to learn the best approach to help. This was now her job. With the exception of the brief training she'd received, she didn't really know how to handle this kind of family. *I'll figure it out*, she told herself.

Now, she wondered just who Juan Martinez really was. Another bad actor? *Careful now, Cameron; go slow, think. Just take it easy.* That always worked for her. She knew she shouldn't discount Judge Crowe; her recommendation based on Juan's behavior was spot-on, but there was only so much she could do.

For the rest of the afternoon, she labored through the other cases before Judge Crowe, but her thoughts were never far from her concerns about Elijah and his mother.

Chapter 4

A NEW CASE

By the time she left the courtroom that afternoon, Cameron had wrapped up the easier cases but couldn't stop thinking about Alisha and Elijah. Cases like this always made her start questioning whether child welfare was really the right field for her. But she didn't want to quit, either. Not yet. She reminded herself that her caseload was balanced with eighteen children; that her supervisor, John Quint, always gave her a hand when needed; and that she was more or less up to date with paperwork, which was always a pain and a frequent subject of complaint by bureaucrats at the DCF.

Cameron was no different from others in the child welfare arena. Everyone knew it was difficult to resuscitate dysfunctional homes, to try to keep children with a parent who was able to care for them. She felt particularly uncomfortable with the attorney for the state in Elijah's case, who had said nothing other than to agree with Attorney Burt. Who was he, anyway? In her experience, attorneys of the state were often inexperienced, unhelpful, and out of touch with the real facts. She knew they never had time to learn the facts or sit with caseworkers and explore details. Even if they were well-intentioned, their caseloads were heavy. She got that. But regardless of what the judge had concluded, Cameron told herself that whatever was happening with Alisha and Elijah Santeroa was not good.

Traffic was heavy on this hot summer afternoon, and Cameron's car was old. The air-conditioning was weak to nonexistent, and driving in traffic was hectic and overwhelming.

She tried distracting herself by thinking about Nick. Nick had shown up in Tampa, rented a cheap garage apartment, and befriended Daniel, who was part of Cameron's group of friends who hung out, texted each other, and made trips to the beach. Daniel was fun—but Nick was different. Cameron wanted to get to know him better. Now, hot and sweaty in a beat-up car, she decided to text Daniel to find out what was going on.

After turning into her office parking lot, she parked and texted Daniel, who immediately texted back that a group of them was planning on a get-together that evening. It wasn't the weekend, but so what? Better to start off the week with some fun. Cameron texted back that she'd see him there. Now she was sure to run into Nick too.

In the downstairs lobby of her office was the usual range of clientele: White, Black, Brown, poor, rich, educated, illiterate. Every time Cameron walked through that lobby, she witnessed a cauldron of relentless problems. That was the hard part. People were not there voluntarily. They were pulled to her office by their families, the courts, the police, and state investigators. It was an endless stream, and the particulars of each situation were always different.

Once she reached the office, she went to her cubicle, tapped the button of her computer to open a table of cases, and thought about her upcoming paperwork. Her cubicle allowed her some privacy but wasn't the same as having an office with a door. It offered three half-walls that allowed her to stare at her computer or her pictures and keepsakes with her back turned to whatever was happening behind her. She loved the picture of her little sister, Rosie, who had a learning disability. Cameron understood and empathized with Rosie and had always protected her and loved teaching her things. There was a picture of her parents and one of Cameron and her older brother, Samuel.

Her superior, John Quint, was in a cubicle adjacent to hers. To talk with Cameron, he simply rolled his chair backward and peered around the corner. This was exactly what he did when Cameron returned to the office that afternoon. Popping his head around the cubicle, he asked, "How was court? Any problems?" He looked at Cameron with his friendly, unassuming smile.

"Not really," she said. "Just the regular, legal beagle stuff." She turned her chair halfway toward him and smiled.

"Want to talk more about it?" he asked. Cameron thought he was often ready to jawbone about the drama of her caseload, along with her mixed feelings about work. She liked that, but now she hesitated, thinking that maybe she should dig back into her paperwork like a good office worker.

When she didn't answer, John stepped around his cubicle. "Sorry, but we have a new case. Judge Crowe again," he said. "The sheriff's investigator sheltered a kid late this afternoon. Child's name is David Williams, three years old. I talked to the deputy sheriff who put him into temporary shelter—maybe will reunite tomorrow with his mother."

"Is this another case of temporary overnight care where an infant is thrown into an office building with an air mattress?" Cameron asked, turning her chair all the way around to face John, crossing her legs and throwing up her hands. She knew she sounded irritated. "I can never get this paperwork done. How about a break?" She stared at John for a few seconds while he looked at her quizzically. She dropped her head and said, "Okay, I get it, sorry. I'm not sure why I'm so crabby. The hearing before Crowe didn't help." John nodded sympathetically; he'd listened to Cameron complain about the judge before.

She shifted her focus to the new case he'd just mentioned. "Is Denitra the sheriff's investigator? Must be a real problem. Maybe you're going to owe me on this one."

"Yeah, I guess I will. It's Denitra and her partner, another deputy sheriff. You could call them—maybe drive over and visit if you want. It'll take some time." John held out some documents and added, "I'll pitch in."

"Okay, you're in. Let's go." She grabbed the documents and charged forward, thinking that it would be a good break to get her mind off court. She picked up her keys. "I'll drive."

"Well, that answers that," John said, laughing.

"Put a bit of energy into it, old man. Hustle, hustle!" Cameron shouted back at him. They jokingly fought to see who would be first to get to the car.

Chapter 5

ANOTHER SHELTERED CHILD

John explained the case while Cameron drove them to the sheriff's office where Denitra worked. The car was blisteringly hot. During the summer, every sitting car in Tampa was white-hot, whether the windows were rolled up or down.

"This isn't really a new case," John said. "The mother is a Sandra Williams. She herself was in foster care her entire life and is still in the DCF system. An addict, clean now. She's under the independent living program, aged into it at nineteen, and for the most part is on her own."

Cameron stared through the windshield, swerving to avoid a reckless driver. "Typical. What else?"

"Apartment neighbor called this morning saying Sandra's child—David's a three-year-old—was sitting on an outdoor walkway, second floor, alone. The door to his mother's apartment was open. Denitra picked up the boy and took him to the temporary shelter of DCF."

Swerving again, Cameron said, "Do you think the kid walked out there, opened the door? Do you think the door was left open? How did this happen?"

"Hard to believe, but how else would he get there? Maybe someone broke in and left the door open. A neighbor looked in and the mother was gone. The file shows that Sandra worked her case plan, did pretty well. Her case manager is out on vacation. We both know the situation: young mother still in the system, her child now in the system too, round and round."

Cameron floored the gas and sped around another car. "Who's the caseworker?"

"Across the hall in the other unit. She's good. Patricia. Cam, are you okay? Am I about to die in a car accident? What's up with you?"

"Patricia? I like her. I don't really know anything about her, I mean professionally. Yeah, I'm okay. Just relax and enjoy the hot ride." She glanced over at John, who had a tight hold on his seat and door. She smiled. He gritted his teeth and squinted his eyes.

They arrived at the office of the sheriff's investigation bureau, which was strictly governmental minimalist. Most everyone wore a deputy sheriff's uniform, and some were standing and talking to each other around cubicles. At least it was a large space: wide open, with big windows and incoming sunlight, not gray or drab. The one picture of an old man in uniform, holding some type of award or plaque, was literally the only decoration on what must have been a hundred-foot wall.

Cameron and John exchanged hellos with Denitra and her fellow deputy sheriff. They walked into an all-glass conference room—not exactly a place for privacy—feeling the eyes of everyone in the office.

Denitra talked as she walked. "We had no choice but to shelter. The kid was out on a second-floor landing unsupervised. The mother never showed up. We waited for an hour. I looked over the child's file after I got back to the office."

DCF had a statewide computer network commonly called FinCen, which contained a file on each child and family within the system. So long as paperwork was entered daily, up-to-date information was available throughout the state's network. Caseworkers were often blamed for late or missing data—typical of DCF, as Cameron well knew.

Denitra continued. "Patricia Smith is the mother's case manager. FinCen says Sandra, the mother, is working under a court plan: parenting, baby care, anger management, no drugs—typical stuff. Drugs were a problem but supposedly no longer. No physical abuse. One interesting entry mentions a Jack Wilson. Patricia is looking into who this guy is, but the file is weak on information. Nothing really. Seems like every case has some guy lurking in the background."

Cameron looked up. "Another *paramour* case," she said, referring to the legal term used for partners of a child's parent or guardian. "I hate that word—can't we come up with something else, like *boyfriend, girlfriend, lover, tramp?*"

"I get it. Believe me, I'm in your corner, but let's keep on track," Denitra said.

Denitra had been a deputy sheriff for ten years and held the rank of corporal in the sheriff's bureau for investigation of child abuse or neglect. Experienced and dedicated, but, like Cameron, she could have an attitude—of course, who didn't? No one was kidding themselves about changing the culture and realities of the American underside. Looking a little old for her thirty-eight years, Denitra had splotchy skin and wore no makeup; she was slim but imposing, dressed in the sheriff's uniform of tan pants and a no-nonsense simple white shirt with built-up shoulders. Cameron and John contested nothing she said.

"Looks like Patricia is working the case pretty good," Denitra went on. "She believes in the mother, who seems to be making progress. Lots of notes in DCF's FinCen; skimpy on detail but a well-written case plan—good notes, which we all know isn't necessarily the usual." She raised her eyebrows, tilting back in her chair and lifting her arms wide with a look of skepticism. Cameron didn't respond to this.

"Cam, John, we need to drill down a bit and figure out the good and bad of this case. Patricia is no novice. I get that. We don't need kids in care, either institutional or foster. I get that. Must be something to Pat's thoughts—keeping the child and mother together. I guess Pat is still on vacation."

John answered quickly. "Two weeks of vacation."

Cameron said nothing. John looked over at her and tilted his head a few times toward her, clearly wondering why she wasn't speaking up.

"Cameron, I know you've got something to say," Denitra said, looking back and forth between them. "Where do you see this thing going? I assume you guys will pick up the ball in court tomorrow—there'll be a shelter hearing for sure." State law required a shelter hearing before a judge within twenty-four hours of removing a child into state care.

Cameron said, "I listened to all of that. Still, like, I don't know anything. How'd David end up on a second-floor landing unattended?"

"Let's get over to Sandra Williams's apartment. Somebody has to be there, or nearby."

"Let's go," Cameron declared.

"Yes, ma'am," said John. "I'm following you today!"

They got into the still-hot car, and Cameron sped off.

Chapter 6

AN ABSENT CHILD

Earlier that day, after Denitra and the deputy sheriff had picked up three-year-old David Williams, they immediately placed him in the youth shelter operated by DCF.

Later, at 6:00 p.m., his mother, Sandra Williams, got to her apartment and discovered that her son was not there. Screaming and yelling, she ran from the apartment and checked with neighbors.

One of her neighbors said, "The state was here and took the kid."

Sandra was furious. "Those motherfucking assholes. Goddamn it! I miss the motherfucking bus and I get no fucking break." She threw up her arms and hurried back to her apartment. Tears flowed, and she threw herself on the floor, head down, and then curled up into a ball, rocking back and forth. "Jesus, Jesus, Jesus."

The neighbor came in and gave her some papers left by Denitra—papers that notified her of the shelter hearing the next day before Judge Crowe at 10:00 a.m. Sandra had been before Judge Crowe many times.

That bitch of a judge, she thought. *I'm working my ass off, trying to get a job, and this is what happens. Sorry-ass bus system. Now I got to kiss ass again before that judge. Been there, done that.* She decided to call her caseworker, Patricia, in the morning. Eventually she got up off the floor and went outside to sit on the apartment steps to escape the heat.

Everything was hot and messy around Sandra's apartment complex in Suitcase City, where the residents were students, the unemployed, those working two to three jobs, drug users—those making ends meet week to week, month to month. Do-gooders and social service agencies plied their trades with inch-by-inch advances, working at social outreach centers, schools, and a few scattered churches. It was a transient place, and neighbors hardly knew each other.

Sandra had some education and remembered a little of what she had learned; she could speak well but favored slang and vulgarity, a nice release for anger and fear. She knew the streets and could work the system. She'd lost David before, and she would stick with the program, notwithstanding her tantrum; stay with Patricia; and get her child back. She was a mother. She accepted her past with drugs and never had much work, but she believed in survival and had strong instincts. The hard things were the temptations. She knew she needed help and guidance. She always got to the court hearings on her son's case early, told her story, and relied on Patricia. She wasn't going to let that bus schedule screw up her life. She'd worked through all the programs on child-rearing, anger management, and drug rehab. She had done it all.

Glancing down the stairwell to the first floor, she noticed the slight figure of a man wearing loose-fitting pants and a tight, stretched, white T-shirt. He was walking toward her and up the stairs. *Shit*, she thought. It was Jack Wilson.

"Hey, didn't think I'd make it, did you?" He strutted up to her with his skinny hips, muscular shoulders, and wide, bright smile. "You're looking good," he remarked, and then changed his tune when he saw Sandra's face. "No, you're looking weirded out."

"They took David," she said.

"Yeah, I wondered where the little shithead was."

Sandra turned her head away.

"Whoa now, don't look away when your man is talking," he said. "I got other things I can do. You know I like David: I go to the park, show him the ropes, feed him. I'm good. You're a lucky bitch—show some respect."

She told him the story. Maybe he'd go to court with her tomorrow.

"No way," he said. "I'm not going to see a judge. Are you crazy? I got no friends downtown. You go alone. Let's watch TV. What beer you got? I got some stuff, but I'm holdin' it for a special occasion."

"I'm good, forget it," Sandra said.

Laughing and shaking his head in disbelief, Jack said, "I won't give up. I'm patient. Just cool down, that's what I want."

They headed into the apartment and closed the door despite the evening's breeze. The apartment was muggy. Doors were normally open in the early evening hours during the hot Tampa summer weather and temperate springs and falls. Soon they heard a knock on the door.

Jack opened the door to a woman and man who stood there facing him directly. Jack didn't approve of what he saw: two professional-looking people, wearing pleated slacks and shined leather shoes. Police, inspectors—anyone like that looked like authority to him. He backed up, still holding the door open with his left hand, and then faced them with his body turned sideways.

"Whoa, who are you?"

"I'm Cameron Springer," the young woman said. "This is John Quint. We're caseworkers on behalf of the Department of Children and Families. Here's our IDs. We're looking for Sandra Williams."

Jack hollered back into the apartment, "Sandra, this is yours." He dropped his hand from the door and headed straight into a back room of the apartment, leaving the door open. Sandra looked out at Cameron and John from her bedroom door and then rushed forward with a fearful look on her face.

Chapter 7

FALLING APART

Before Cameron and John knocked on the door of Sandra Williams's apartment, but after they had spoken with Denitra about Sandra and her child, they gave some thought to the next day's shelter hearing before Judge Crowe. They knew Patricia was diligent and reliable. She had obviously vouched for Sandra, or David would have been taken to shelter long before that day. On the other hand, it was also obvious that the case was odd and troubling given the fact that David, a three-year-old, was sitting alone on the outside landing of a second-floor apartment. Something was screwy.

From Cameron's viewpoint, the decision to visit Sandra had been forced on her. She was not in the mood to walk into court the next day. Enough was enough. Surely a different judge would be taking shelter hearings. Having thought all of that, she nevertheless showed up with John and knocked on Sandra's door.

The apartment complex was a typical garden style: three stories, with every front door facing an outside landing or balcony. There was a small courtyard. It was nothing fancy: concrete block construction, metal railings and fencing on the outside of each upper-floor landing. Some residents kept plants or flowers on the landings, but most didn't. Like the neighborhood in general, residents were transitory for the most part. The complex had no built-in AC units. Cameron and John stood out, just as they had at sheriff headquarters, maybe because they were young.

When Jack Wilson answered the door, Cameron and John were relieved—at least someone was home. With an open door, Cameron and John observed Wilson as a lanky, muscular young man in his early twenties with a streetwise look about him, tattoos on his forearms of blue arrows surrounded and almost covered by purple flowers, pierced ears, and bright blue but sullen eyes.

Under these circumstances, Cameron was glad to have John with her, even though he was the exact opposite—not physically intimidating or street tough. John was skinny and medium height, wearing rumpled, pleated trousers, a button-down collared shirt, and Sunday school shoes. He was good at reading books—not so good at physical confrontations. Cameron couldn't even conceive of a tough version of John. He was just a small Irishman, for God's sake! *Give him a break*, she thought. She was thankful he was there with her now.

Sandra ran forward wearing a summer skirt and a loose, long-sleeved blouse over strong, curvy shoulders, and no shoes—a typical Florida look for a hot evening. She stood in stark contrast to Cameron's light-colored capris, sandals, and rose-colored blouse, its sleeves cut short. Cameron's darker skin glowed beneath the early evening sunlight still beaming through a window. It had been a long day, but she felt loose and ready to engage.

Sandra immediately collapsed, crying and laying her head flat against the linoleum floor, arms splayed out in front of her, sobbing, trying to talk. Between gulps of air and exhausted moans, she groaned, "I'm trying, I'm trying, God help me, help me!"

John kept his hands in his back pockets, head cocked to his right side with a frown. Jack Wilson had already fled, slamming the door. Cameron crouched down and touched Sandra lightly. "All right, all right," she said, her hands on Sandra's shoulders.

After a few minutes, Sandra sat up on the floor and faced Cameron. Cameron was quiet, guiding her to a chair. "Let me know when you're ready to talk, ready to listen," she said. She sat on a beat-up couch beside Sandra.

"The bus was late. I got home late. I was supposed to be home at 4:00. I promised the neighbor I would be home then, but the bus was late. Don't think I got the job anyway. The neighbor must not have watched him. Please don't take David. Is he okay? Where is he? It hurts so much." She had stopped crying but still made rough, guttural sounds.

"He's fine," Cameron said. "He's in the shelter. No problems. You could have called your caseworker, Pat, for a ride." For a second, she forgot that Pat was away.

"I did, but she's on vacation. I tried. I'm trying to get that job."

"Let's talk about what's going on," Cameron said. So they talked.

John listened, but his mind drifted to different places and different times. He had summed up the situation quickly once he saw Jack Wilson. He figured Sandra was headed down a lost road and would probably end up in a gutter of meth, heroin, crack—whatever. He didn't want to think that his mind was closed. Even so, he had the experiences, ones he couldn't overlook.

Cameron was the opposite. For all her steely objectivity and practiced discipline to be stoic and realistic in the midst of a crisis, inside she felt touched by Sandra. Cameron wasn't thinking of drugs, hopelessness, and despair, or of uncertainties and the stress of court hearings. She tried to comfort Sandra. She listened to her.

This was her way. The courtroom was uncertain in terms of results and always prompted nerves, but for some reason this kind of situation was calming for Cameron. Maybe it was a feeling that she was doing something helpful, something right, something real. For all her lack of control over Sandra's situation in that moment, Cameron was filled with empathy. It came to her as naturally as did support for her sister, Rosie.

"We will deal with that tomorrow—I'll be there with you and the judge," Cameron assured Sandra. "Patricia is out for now. Let's talk about a game plan, something that will work for you and David."

John knew Cameron had planned to meet friends that evening—which now probably wouldn't happen. No wonder she struggled with friendships, he thought. She was always caught up in her cases. But then again, so was he; he wasn't a nightlife kind of guy. He knew he shouldn't be thinking about it, but he had been attracted to Cameron since the first day she showed up at the office, and watching her talk with Sandra, he felt that pull again.

Cameron often spoke to mothers with reassurance. This mother was pleading for the power and strength to go on. He felt sad for Sandra. On the other hand, in his experience, this type of interaction sometimes proved to be manipulative. He began to feel uncomfortable. *Let's get on with it*, he thought. *Call it for what it is and move on. For instance, where is Jack? How does he fit in with this?* A live-in or drop-by or, better put, a dropout? John suspected that Sandra was faking it—he'd seen plenty of acts before.

His big moment as a caseworker had been the rescue of a ten-year-old boy from a father. No mother was in the home. The boy had happened to call the DCF child abuse hotline, and John got the assignment. He rescued the boy that afternoon. He went with deputy sheriffs to a sagging mobile home next to an overgrown lake—oaks covered in Spanish moss, loads of mosquitos—with a dirt drive about a quarter mile off the road, no neighbors to be seen. The kid wasn't in the system, so there were no prior referrals, but it sounded like he must have been in school. He knew how to dial a phone number. John banged on the door, and the boy opened it. There were bruises on one arm and one eye. When he saw the investigator's sheriff's van, the boy cried out, "Help me, help!" and started sobbing. He bolted out of the trailer and yanked on the door of the sheriff's van. In that case, the court proceedings were swift, and John got the boy out of the home and into a shelter, terminated parental rights, and moved the boy into a workable foster home and finally into adoption.

John grew up in Orlando and graduated from the University of Central Florida with a degree in social sciences, like Cameron's field of study. A good student, he volunteered as manager of an intercollegiate wrestling team. He had some girlfriends and liked going to parties and bars, but he was always in the background. He'd talk baseball to anyone who would listen. His main activity was watching baseball on TV. In a bar, he could sit there and watch a game from beginning to end without interruption. He liked the Tampa Bay Rays but had never been to a real game.

He started work in Tampa with DCF for a couple of years and later transferred over to Kids Care. At this point he had worked there for four years, having started as an intern before moving into casework and then up the chain to supervisor. He liked rules, the meetings with social workers, and even liked all the paperwork that seemed a mystery to everyone else in the office. He kept the latest professional articles and reports at his fingertips and was excellent at citing scholarly information. Fieldwork wasn't his thing, but he was good at it, and he knew when to defer to others. Cameron was a perfect working partner for him—but as he had to admit, watching her now, that seemed to be as deep as their relationship would ever go.

John didn't participate in the back-and-forth between Cameron and Sandra. He stood next to the front door the entire time. He decided to let Cameron provide support and get Sandra calmed down. Once they knew she was safe, they could leave. But as he stood there waiting, he realized he was seeing something off with Sandra—he didn't believe her.

Chapter 8

A NIGHT OUT

Once Cameron's magic worked, Sandra calmed down. John convinced Cameron that they could safely leave, and that Sandra would be able to keep it together.

They drove back to the office and said their goodbyes. Cameron was alone by 9:30 p.m. Now what to do? *God*, she thought, *I haven't touched base with any of my friends. This work is killing me.* She grabbed her cell phone.

As organized by Daniel, a group was gathering at Sam's, a comfortable, slightly shabby hangout with good, cold beer and tasty fried food. Daniel and Nick were sure to be there.

Cameron enjoyed hanging out with guys—the fun of friendly repartee, the back-and-forth banter and flirtation. She enjoyed being the center of attention. In high school, she had been shy and reserved, but college had brought out her personality. There, she had two romances. The first ended on friendly and innocent terms, but the second was intense, the ending hard. She retreated into herself. Eventually she got over it, but it left her with a wary eye that crept into any growing male friendship. Now and then she wondered how she would end up, but mostly she could laugh about it.

But she didn't laugh about her work. The uncertainties surrounding her cases never eased. Whenever one case closed and dropped out of her mind, a new one took its place.

She admired her parents and often thought of her sister, Rosie: she was eighteen years old now, but she would always be dependent on her parents. Cameron admired their commitment, and her own relationship with her special sister was a source of strength and justification for what she was doing with her life. *Steadfast.* It was how she thought of her family and herself.

As she ducked back into her car for the drive to Sam's at the end of a trying day, Cameron's thoughts drifted into the world of three-year-old David Williams, a world that seemed to include his mother's friend Jack Wilson. What was he about? He certainly didn't seem to be a cornerstone to building a secure life. Exactly how did Sandra's relationship with Jack Wilson work with Sandra's son, David? Sitting in her car, she sent an email to John: *I'm not comfortable with the boyfriend, or whatever that Jack guy is. Thoughts? Run a profile through law enforcement, u think?*

That done, she shifted to the thought that she might run into Mr. Wonderful tonight but almost immediately told herself to calm down and not get ahead of herself. Her car was still steamy from the day. She turned on the radio and listened to a tune by Hootie and the Blowfish. She liked that folksy, intimate sound out of South Carolina—not that she was turning Southern, that was for sure, but she liked it.

It seemed everyone was at Sam's. Nick was in the corner, talking with some guys she didn't know. She bumped into Daniel and got a bear hug and a kiss to the ear—nice, brotherly, warm. They faced the group with arms wrapped around each other. She felt comfortable with

Daniel. There was plenty of laughter and salutations, and thoughts of Alisha, Sandra, Elijah, and David vanished.

Cameron wasn't overly caught up with her outfit or her looks, even though her face wasn't exactly fresh as the morning dew. Her eyes were bleary and tinged a bit red, and her face was a little pasty from a long, trying day, but the light was dark inside Sam's, so that didn't matter. Her smile was big—a tired, through-the-mill, relieved, and happy look.

Sam's was hot and humid too. It was a sexy place: loads of young, raging hormones loosely dressed, everyone sweaty as on any Tampa Bay summer evening. But the AC did work, off and on. And the smell was raw.

Daniel unwrapped his arms, and Cameron scooted off to chat with her friend Grace.

"Tough day?" Grace asked.

"Yeah," Cameron said. "A long day, just need to relax. I guess I'm used to it. I promised myself in the car I'd let it go, maybe find Mr. Wonderful tonight. Not sure that's happening. Do you like judges?"

"What?" Grace answered. "Are you playing with me? There are lots of Mr. Wonderfuls here. So lighten up, Cam. We're not going to have a serious session tonight of *what's life all about*. And you know I don't know anything about judges. I don't know one and don't *want* to know one."

"No, no, sorry, Grace! Forget about it, okay?"

Grace smiled at her and changed the subject. "You look good, Cam."

"Yeah, under the circumstances I do look good!" Cameron said. "Thanks for the compliment. I'm beat. Let's go have some fun!"

Grace said, "Look, I visited a construction site and bossed around some old guys today. Believe it or not, that already was fun." Grace was a civil engineer and worked as a construction manager.

"Your job is concrete—okay, bad pun—but you know what I mean. You see improvement and then it finishes."

Grace shrugged. "My job can be hard, too. At least you're helping people, while I'm looking over a concrete pour."

"You know, it is what it is. I don't want to complain too much, not right now; we've got jobs, and, like I said, let's have some fun. Save our troubles for the phone, when we can talk each other into some sleep. Look at Nick over there in a corner. I'm going over there. Where's Daniel?"

"He's wedged into the bar with a bunch of guys," Grace said. "I'll save him." She headed into the bar mix and took over the conversation. She looked good too, dressed in long, tight yoga pants with a colorful top. Her hair was long and blond with highlights.

Cameron brazenly interrupted Nick's conversation—something about the 2008 economic crash, the Federal Reserve, interest rates, and Ben Bernanke, the bigwig at the reserve.

"Hi, I'm Cameron," she said, holding out her hand to the friend, who shook it and said, "I can't compete with that, Nick! See you. I'm out of here." He turned around and shot back a thumbs-up to Nick.

Daniel and Grace walked over. The four of them ordered some beers and for an hour or so engaged in light banter about movies, TV, their friends, and experiences they'd had in other cities. Cameron bailed out first, saying, "Okay, guys, thanks for the fun, but I'm beat. Catch you later. I had fun. Grace, call me."

Cameron drove back to her apartment in West Tampa, an old immigrant neighborhood inhabited by Cubans and Spanish, with a few Italians mixed in. For sixty years they'd come to Tampa to work in cigar factories and east of the city to work on tomato and strawberry farms. Now, with cigars a dead industry and virtually all work shipped out to the Caribbean and Central and South America, the cigar factories stood as silent, physical ghosts of things past, left empty for decades without any attention or rehabilitation. West Tampa remained dominated by vestiges of those earlier times. But some development had begun to sprout up in the wake of their departure, starting with four-story apartment buildings with gated entrances—small units attractive to the young, like Cameron, and all of it made more attractive by the remaining relics.

Her apartment was on the second floor of one of the newer buildings. She had a bedroom and one main room for the kitchen, living room, and dining area—nothing fancy, but it worked for her. She crawled into bed, happy to be there, thinking about the fun at Sam's—and then, in the back of her mind, she thought of Sandra and David Williams and the shelter hearing the next day before Judge Crowe.

Chapter 9

PURPLE TATTOOS

Cameron went to the office early the next morning, Tuesday, a little foggy but chipper. It had helped to have some fun at Sam's the night before, and she'd had a better-than-usual night of sleep.

"Good morning!" she said to John. "How about we chat in about ten minutes? Give me some time to check into my computer and get going."

"Fine," he replied. In addition to his suppressed physical attraction, John truly liked talking to Cameron—it was a feeling of comfort in a job with plenty of downsides. He felt she trusted him, and he knew he trusted her. Today they needed to prepare for the shelter hearing at 10:00 a.m. for Sandra and her son.

After ten minutes, he pulled his chair around to Cameron's cubicle. "I got in early and pulled up criminal records on Jack Wilson," he told her. "Nothing terrible, but he's got an assortment of little stuff: arrests starting early on, probably going back even further, petty theft, DUI, possession of stolen property—nothing physical. He was in foster care;

that's no big surprise. I pulled up his case file: typical stuff, parents on drugs, poverty, in and out of family and foster care. Dropped out of school. Probably sells. He's twenty-two. I couldn't find his address, but he must hang out somewhere. He's not in any independent-living program and not getting money from the state."

Cameron leaned back in her chair, listening but also thinking that John wasn't bad looking, though maybe a bit too skinny. As far as she knew, he was single. He was no Nick, not even a Daniel. And it was definitely obvious he liked women. "So where do we start?" she said. "Who was his last caseworker?"

"Susan somebody; I haven't heard of her. He was assigned to a different agency, not ours. She doesn't seem to be in the system anymore."

"Let's check with his last probation officer, maybe the public defender on the petty theft charge. Why don't we hit the street to try and run this thing down? It'd get us out of the office."

John smiled at the idea of another road trip with Cameron; maybe he could finagle a lunch and have some fun. He relaxed back in his chair. "Yeah, maybe have some fun. We can call a probation officer. And later maybe get some lunch in West Tampa—a good Cuban sandwich with some black beans. I'm going to hit the head. See you at the elevator." He hopped up and started down the hall.

"You know I have to be in court at 10:00 for the hearing on the Williams case," Cameron shouted at him.

He kept on walking. "Yeah, I know," he said, turning his head back toward Cameron.

It turned out that the probation officer didn't know too much, but he did say that Jack Wilson hung out in Seminole Heights, an older neighborhood in Tampa, north of downtown. Seminole Heights had seen better days in the 1940s and '50s. Wilson stayed with some friends in Seminole Heights off Twenty-Second Street, at times around a corner near Thirtieth Street. The officer named a sister. They located an address for her in the same neighborhood.

Seminole Heights took its name from an offshoot of Florida's Seminole Indian history. "Heights" had some truth to it: it was a piece of geography relatively high compared to the sea level of Tampa Bay.

Cameron and John ended up driving separately and arrived at the sister's address and knocked on the door. A young woman answered. Cameron produced identification, explaining that they were investigating a child welfare matter and that in the process they had run across her brother, Jack Wilson.

"I don't know Jack Wilson," the woman responded. She was medium height, dressed in black short-shorts and a tank top. She was barefoot. She was dusty, as if she worked with clay and pottery.

"Isn't he your brother?" John asked. "We can always come back. Talk to your neighbors."

"Yeah, so what, I don't know a Jack Wilson. I ran across a guy named Jay Wilson," she said. "I don't have any brother alive."

John continued. "What does this Jason look like? I mean Jay."

"Dirty, light-brown hair, medium height, not fat, not skinny. White—real white—with blue and purple tattoos on his forearms. Weird-looking tattoos. Muscular, big shoulders."

"What's he do?"

"I don't know."

"He has money, doesn't he? I mean in his pockets, cash?" John pressed.

"Sometimes."

"Where's he now? You know, don't you? This is important."

"No," she said, scowling. "Why are you getting so pushy? I'm going inside. I'm working; I don't care about my neighbors." She slammed the door and barked, "You're no cop, leave me alone." She left Cameron and John standing there, looking at each other. John made a contorted face and remarked, "That was a lot of nothing." Cameron pressed her lips together and frowned, and then she turned and walked back to her car. John followed.

"Oh well," Cameron said to John with a shrug as she got in her car. "So be it."

After they left, Cameron took off for the courthouse. She expected Sandra would be in court and figured that if her bad luck held over from yesterday, there would be some lawyer sitting beside Sandra, together with a court-appointed guardian for David and the attorney for the state. They would know nothing about the case. *I don't know anything either, except the smell of it*, she thought. *But here I go, back to the courtroom for more fireworks with Judge Crowe.*

On a lark, John headed to Twenty-Second Street. He'd gotten a kick out of confronting Jack Wilson's so-called sister, had a bit of an adrenaline rush, and decided to see if he could learn anything else.

He picked a bar on a corner and went inside—and immediately ran into Jack Wilson. The bar was pitch-black. Jack stood out, light from an open door reflecting off his white skin. The tattoos. *Now what?* John wondered. *I'm a social worker, not a cop.* But he couldn't just run away; the guy was right in front of him. So he approached him and asked him to please come outside for a minute. Jack looked at him skeptically but followed.

Outside, Wilson asked, "Are you insane or just stupid? You trying to get killed or get made, or trying to get me killed? You're not helping me or Sandra. I'm not your friend, and you got no business with me."

John watched a guy walk by as Wilson said to him, "What's happening, Striker? Check you later." Then, turning back to John, he said, "Man, I don't know you and don't want to. Get out of here."

"Mr. Wilson, I will be back, and you can expect I'll need to know more about you," John said. "This is just about David Williams, nothing else, and I need to know your involvement." *Where did that come from?* he wondered.

Wilson put his hands in his front pockets, pushed his chest out, and pulled his shoulders back, looking ready to take a swipe at John. "Get!" he said. John turned and left.

John found his car and drove off. This level of activity for him was extraordinary. He knew himself to be nerdy, an intellectual at best, and was dumbstruck by his own actions. It just wasn't like him to confront someone like that. But he had a funny feeling, too: he had *liked* it.

Chapter 10

ANOTHER DAY IN COURT

Cameron settled into the courtroom. A few minutes later, Judge Crowe arrived, sat down at her courtroom desk, and said good morning. Then she called up the first case on the docket. Cameron imagined that this was the routine the judge followed every morning: there was the printout of her caseload for the day to review, which would include the status of each case's preparation, notes on pretrial conferences, recommendations on whether a parent should lose custody of his or her child, and shelter hearings for children taken into custody the day before.

The shelter hearing for David Williams was one of thirty cases that day—each scheduled for no more than ten minutes. It was going to be a nine-to-ten-hour day in the courtroom. Normally the day would run from 9:00 a.m. to 4:30 p.m., with an hour and a half for lunch, but today was a cattle call.

On a day like this, Cameron knew, with the number of cases to get through, the odds were strong that Judge Crowe would have no specific recollection of David or of his mother. David wasn't present at the hearing, but Sandra Williams was. The state, as usual, was represented by an assistant attorney from the state attorney general's office, a different one from yesterday. Everyone in the courtroom was dressed in some type of ordinary suit, except for Sandra, who was wearing jeans and a plain white blouse.

Caseworkers like Cameron explained situations and circumstances. Attorneys for the state usually offered up nothing in particular. Judges asked questions seeking assurance that each kid was safe and that the parent was following the case plan. Most cases shuffled along in ten minutes, but that could drag on if any controversy or meaningful question arose.

Judge Crowe reached David's case at 11:00 a.m., an hour behind schedule. She turned to Cameron and asked for a summary. Cameron explained events of the previous day, and Sandra Williams offered nothing to the contrary.

"I'm recommending that the court release David from temporary shelter back to the custody of his mother," Cameron said. In a good mood after her evening out, Cameron wanted to present this case as matter-of-factly as possible. She still had an instinct that something was off with Jack Wilson, but she didn't expand on that and kept to the basic facts. While she spoke, the assistant attorney remained silent. Cameron may not have been a lawyer, but she did know that the assistant attorney just didn't know the facts, and he hadn't been there the night before.

Judge Crowe stated to Cameron, "Ms. Springer, let me get this straight. David Williams, a three-year-old, was on a second-floor landing alone and had been there for some time. Is that correct?"

"Yes, your honor, that's my understanding."

That said, Cameron finished her presentation. Given the judge's ruling the day before in favor of the reunification of Alisha and Elijah, she figured her arguments for relying on a well-intentioned mother weren't out of left field, although she was well aware the judge wasn't happy with the details. It was then time for Judge Crowe to decide. She hesitated. Cameron knew that the judge tended to think that paramour cases required more information. But that had had little to do with her ruling the day before concerning Elijah Santeroa, and Cameron had been careful not to elaborate beyond what she absolutely knew about Jack Wilson.

Judge Crowe decided to bore down into the matter. Had there been a review of the criminal records for any arrest and conviction of Jack Wilson? Yes, they had run a criminal background check; there was nothing physical, no guns involved, just petty theft–type stuff. Was Jack Wilson employed? Cameron stated that that was not known.

Maybe it was something in her tone, but Cameron's uncertainties about Wilson were coming out. After several more minutes of questioning, the judge said, "Let's keep David in temporary custody for a few more days. I'll permit unsupervised visitation by his mother but only at the temporary shelter, while we learn more about Wilson."

At this, Sandra broke down in tears and the bailiff escorted her out of the courtroom. She was virtually collapsing again, this time in the bailiff's arms. She turned and looked pleadingly toward Cameron, who looked sadly at Sandra as she was escorted out.

Cameron then turned back to the judge and sat quietly with an expression of bewilderment. How had this happened? Yesterday Judge Crowe had ordered Elijah home, but now she was ordering David to stay in the state's care—both directly contradicting Cameron's recommendations. Was she doing something wrong? There was always a winner and a loser in court; Cameron knew that. But she was having trouble figuring out what the judge was thinking.

As Judge Crowe shuffled her papers for the next case, Cameron gathered her own things to leave. She looked to the state attorney sitting next to her and said, "Well, that's just too sad. This is going to need some special attention. So I'll be back on this."

The attorney responded, "Cameron, that's fine; I'll be around. Yeah, it's sad. Nothing new, of course—it's always sad."

Cameron walked out to the parking lot to her stifling car, feeling like she'd failed Sandra and Daniel. She just couldn't figure out how Judge Crowe had decided to dismiss her recommendations for two cases in a row. How was she troubled about Jack Wilson but not troubled by Juan Martinez, Alisha Santeroa's friend? What exactly was the difference between the two?

Chapter 11

THE DOCKS AND A BAR

After his encounter with Jack Wilson, John scooted south on Twenty-Second Street toward the docks of Tampa Bay and a stevedore union hall, thinking he might get some information on Juan Martinez. Alisha had said he worked at the docks, so he figured he'd find out.

At the union hall he got nothing; no one would tell him anything, citing privacy issues. He then headed to another bar near the docks, figuring he could hang out at lunchtime, maybe gather some relevant information. The bar was raw and dirty and smelled like steel and dock workers' sweat. An old fan hung over an open, stand-up bar worn with scrapes and dents. The floor was a sandy linoleum, lit up by a wall of beer signs and one big window sign saying, "Open."

Dressed in khaki pants, a clean, collared shirt, and loafers, John didn't look the part. He didn't think anyone there was going to speak with him. He'd never thought of himself as a quitter, and he felt like he was on a roll after his experience that morning with Jack Wilson. So what if he had other cases to consider? He'd let those slide for now.

It was 11:00 a.m. The bar was just off the Twenty-Second Street Causeway, which served as a bridge between a large working harbor on the bay and the industrial properties on the east side. People shuffled in and out. John went over to stand at the bar, where he could observe. Some people were at tables, mostly eating fried shrimp and hush puppies. The air was stuffy and humid; the AC worked, but he could hear the compressor outside chugging hard, about to break down any minute.

"I'll have a Budweiser," he said to the bartender, a gruff-looking, overweight, older man in jeans and a Florida tourist shirt that had lots of palm trees and beach sand.

Now what? As John stood there, taking small sips of the beer and munching on Cheetos, he tried to listen to what was going on around him without looking too conspicuous. Aside from a few quick glances in his direction, no one seemed to notice or care that he was there.

Women, cases, money, his future—his mind drifted while he stood there. What was he missing? Did it make sense to be standing here, alone, leaning against a bar? What did he think he was going to find out anyway? Maybe it was a newfound feeling of some type of power, or the adrenaline rush arising from the field investigation in which he found himself presently engaged that kept him at the bar. Not that he knew what to do with it.

Around noon, more people came in—dockworkers and manual laborers, from the look of them. He tried to appear like he was minding his own business, but he listened to conversations. People came and went. He was getting nowhere, he realized. How was he supposed to get a lead on Juan Martinez this way? But he stayed. At 12:30, he finally left. It was time to get back to the office to work up some other cases, maybe go by and check on Alisha Santeroa later in the afternoon, try to get some more information, maybe make some headway.

By the time John got back to the office, Cameron was already there, back from court.

"You won't believe this," she said. "Judge Crowe kept David Williams in custody—totally different from yesterday with Elijah Santeroa. This morning, she keeps the Williams kid in temporary, and yesterday she turns the Santeroa kid over to her mother. I can't figure it out. There's no rhyme or reason."

John sighed. Sure, maybe he'd been deluded to think that he'd actually be able to learn anything about Juan Martinez from his rookie stakeout at the bar. But sometimes Cameron just seemed so young and inexperienced that he felt impatient.

"I just don't get it," Cameron said, looking petulant. "What am I missing?"

John shrugged. "Look, that lawyer showed up for Elijah Santeroa, and it sounds like the judge ruled based on his argument. Anyway, the main elements of both cases aren't anything new: poverty, drugs, bad company—like maybe a bad boyfriend. The judge can't kick out every boyfriend like that she comes across, you know that."

Cameron didn't look convinced.

"And you have to accept that, with twenty years on the bench, Judge Crowe does have the experience to make these decisions. She's been reelected three times, you know. She knows who she can trust for reasonably good judgment, and I'm sure you're in that category. She often listens to you. But they're still her decisions, not yours."

"I know, but—"

"She didn't agree with you," John said, cutting her off. "She sided with Chad Burt. It happens. You're just not going to win them all. And remember, she has plenty of cases to get through. Every day."

Cameron was staring at him. "Well, I guess I asked for it," she said.

"Look, Cam, the kid was out on the second-floor landing alone! What was she supposed to do?"

"Okay, okay, you can back off now. I asked for the lecture. Got it. I do appreciate it. Really."

"Fine," John said, turning around to his cubicle. He scratched his head, laughing to himself. *She's crazy, and maybe I am too.* Some cases just really got to you.

Later that afternoon, Cameron received a call from another of her cases, a mother who needed to pick up her child but couldn't get there. Cameron said she'd pick up the six-year-old at her summer program and get her home. She headed out to the east side of town to the school.

"How was school? Did you have fun?" she asked after strapping the girl into a booster seat in the back of her car. Cameron had different car seats for three ages: newborns, toddlers, and prekindergartners.

"Good!" the girl responded. "We did blocks and paints."

"How are your friends?"

"Who?" The girl was in blue jeans and a colorful cotton shirt with no sleeves. Her hair was light brown, with long curls. Her socks were pink.

"Your friends. Who are they?"

"We kicked the ball. And it didn't rain!"

Cameron smiled to herself and thought, *Kids. They'll tell you what they want to tell you.*

"I'm hungry," the girl said.

"Okay, I have some crackers for you and a juice box. Here you go. Did you mind the teacher? I bet you did. Is she nice?"

"Yep."

"Say 'Thank you,'" Cameron said, handing the juice box to her.

"Thank you."

"You're welcome."

Cameron dropped the child with her mother and headed over to Next Step, a program for parenting, job training, and anger management. She knew a counselor who had worked with Alisha under her case-management plan. Maybe she would know more about Alisha's situation—especially about Juan Martinez—and maybe something about Sandra Williams as well. Cameron had placed Alisha at Next Step as part of her case plan, and her attendance was strong.

Cameron explained that she had serious concerns about Alisha and Sandra. "For some reason, my instincts are telling me there's more to these cases," she said to the counselor. "What do you know?"

The counselor was quick to say she didn't know much. She'd never seen either of them with bruises. They visited her, sober, once every two weeks. Alisha got rides from her mother, and Sandra managed to come up with transportation one way or another. Apparently, she was usually dropped off by an older woman; the counselor didn't know her name and had never actually met her.

"Any little details, suggestions, or maybe just general unhappiness or whatever?" Cameron asked.

"I know what you mean," the counselor said, nodding her head. Sitting at her desk, she said, "You know, truth is that Sandra and Alisha don't talk that much about their love lives, so I don't have anything specific. Alisha did say she had a friend who worked at the docks who was good with Elijah. I tried to draw her out but didn't press it. It's sensitive, you know. I need their confidence."

Cameron thanked her. She was too tired to drill down on Sandra's background any further. Enough was enough for her that day, and back at the office she knew that the paperwork would be mounting.

Chapter 12

ALLIGATORS

As Cameron was driving, John called. She answered, driving with one hand as she talked.

"Hey," she said. "I'm feeling better. Drove a kid from school to her mother—that's a nice break. Can't wait to relax, have some alone time tonight."

"Well, yes, that's nice, but I don't know about that alone time. Pick me up at the office," he said. "I just got another call from Denitra. She has another case, wants us to take a look. She's on her way east of the city, a case out in the tomato fields or cattle country. Doesn't sound good."

"She should bring the kid into shelter. That's normal. Why us? It's interesting, her calling us." John didn't reply, and Cameron was quiet for a few seconds. "Okay, I get it, another one. Wow, the week from hell. See you soon."

Within twenty minutes, Cameron was at the office. John jumped into her car, and they headed to the eastern part of Tampa Bay, an area Cameron hardly knew.

"Tough cases out here," John said. "Meth, opioids. It's always a mess."

The house was a short distance off the main highway, behind a swamp and alligators. There were also cypress trees laden with hanging moss and supporting nests for egrets, ibises, and herons.

"I bet there's snakes in there, you think?" Cameron asked.

"We can count on that. Let's stay clear, not get too inquisitive, if you don't mind."

"No problem," Cameron said. "I'm from New Jersey."

Cameron spotted Denitra and her co-deputy out front, paperwork in hand. They walked over to Cameron and John, reaching them halfway between the car and the house. John reverted to his listening persona. Cameron started talking right away. "This is swampy, and where is the child? Did you see those alligators?"

"Cameron, this is Florida—the sticks," Denitra said. "The child is in the house with the father, mother, and three other kids, ages five to nine. The one daughter is bruised, with a broken shoulder. A three-year-old. We received a call from the tip line and got here about two hours ago. The tip must have come from a hospital. We did a preliminary investigation, talked with the parents. They've been married ten years. He works on a ranch: a real live cowboy, spurs and everything. The mother's in a dazed and zoned-out state; looks like meth maybe. He's kind of belligerent. He's holding on to all his kids, and not too happy. We called a few more officers for backup because we're inclined to take custody of all the kids."

"Okay, I get it," Cameron said. "I'm glad we're here to help out, but should we really be here? We're not supposed to do investigations on the front end and take custody. I mean, I guess there are exceptions."

"Cam, I want you to see this up front because I'm going to make sure you and John have this case to handle. We can't have some neophytes assigned to this one."

John said, "Different, being on the front end of a shelter; that's true.

Denitra, I think we can proceed as you suggest. This is troublesome—I mean the facts. We're dealing with four kids, and only one is hurt. This is based on nothing but a hotline tip. Better to think hard."

"Let's hang around and see," Denitra said. John buried his hands in his back pockets, rocking a little back and forth, shuffling his feet. He glanced at some alligators basking on the side of the dirt road. Cameron walked to her car and leaned against the hood, with her head looking down and her hand on her hip, thinking.

They all stood for what seemed an interminable time. Eventually, Denitra's assistant deputy spoke up. "Cam, I have an idea if you'll walk over here," he said. "Look, the family inside is on the verge of ruin, or at least seemingly so, and it'd be best to pull our thoughts together before backup arrives. How about we get our thinking out in the open? I'm the low man on the totem pole, but how about it?"

"Okay, go for it," Cameron said.

The deputy sheriff continued, "How many times have we seen stuff like this? I'm not in the mood to bust up an entire family right now. I say we go inside and try to get to the bottom of this."

"Easy to say, hard to do," said Cameron. "This is a family unit with parents—not the typical thing we see. Is someone a bad actor? Father, mother, older brother? Not likely anyone is going to fess up. I vote to take the little one with the broken shoulder into custody, based on the hospital report, and then dig in as we go along. It's risky, but the alternative is to take all the kids."

"Safety of the kids is our mission, not family survival," Denitra said.

John spoke up. "Safety is our number one issue. And let's move a little closer to the house. That alligator is over there; he's got to be at least seven feet."

Denitra looked at it and said, "That's a small one. Aren't you from Florida?"

"Yeah, but I'm not a total idiot," John said. They all moved a little closer to the house. "Listen, I would go in and hear them out. That works for me, and then we can discuss and decide."

Cameron looked serious, head cocked and frowning, with both hands now on her hips. She thought for another second and then said, "Let's go inside." Before waiting for an answer from the others, she approached the front door and knocked, and then cracked it open. "We need to talk to you," she said.

The cowboy answered, "Come in."

They found their way to the kitchen, where the mother was seated, head down on her arms on a table. The four kids, including the injured three-year-old, must have been in back in one of the bedrooms.

"I'm a caseworker with Kids Care Inc.," Cameron said to them, "and Ms. Denitra and her partner are deputy sheriffs. I don't normally show up like this, but we want to help. Someone at the hospital must have placed a call to a tip line, and so we're here. We need to get some answers, and then maybe we can find a way to help out. So please give us some cooperation here. Is that okay?"

The cowboy answered, "Yes." So far, he didn't seem that belligerent.

Denitra said, "Thank you. We understand your youngest has a broken shoulder, and we did see that. We also understand she has some bruises on her back. You showed those to us earlier. Now, do you know how this happened?"

"I don't know," the cowboy, Mr. Halstrom, said. "I was at work, came home, saw my daughter, and took her to the hospital. My wife said nothing."

"I don't want to interview the children right now—maybe later sometime—but I'm concerned about your wife. Can you tell me about her?" Denitra asked.

"No."

"You're not helping us with that kind of answer, Mr. Halstrom. Right now she looks incapable of taking care of these children. What do you make of that?"

"I don't make nothing of it. She doesn't feel well; I can see that. She's a good mother and loves these kids. When I got home, things were different with her; I get that. Maybe she needs to be left alone and get some rest. That's what I think. Maybe you should come back tomorrow."

"Can you stay home with them until tomorrow morning?" Denitra asked.

"Yeah, but I got to leave early, at 4:00 in the morning. Things are busy at the ranch."

"Mr. Halstrom, we need to discuss this, so why don't the four of us step outside for another few minutes and then we'll be back to you," said Denitra. The four of them walked outside. Back in their huddle, Denitra explained her confliction. She didn't see any injury to the other three children; based on her experience, they looked safe. She asked the others for their thoughts.

Again, no one said much for a moment, and then Cameron spoke. "This is hard. The big question is the wife. Maybe she's perfectly fine, or maybe he inflicted the injuries, not her. Who knows?"

As they conferred, two sheriff's vehicles showed up with two backup officers. Denitra and her co-deputy brought them up to speed. They leaned against their vehicles, waiting for a decision.

Denitra turned back to Cameron and said she agreed with her: it *was* hard. She asked her co-deputy what he thought.

"I can go with sheltering the injured three-year-old," he said. "The hospital suspected abuse or we never would have heard from the hotline in the first place. We don't have a clear picture, but we do know we have an injured child and no answers. We've got to do something."

"John, what do you think? Are we missing something?" Denitra asked.

"Let's take the injured youngster into shelter," he said. "That's the right way to go for now." Cameron couldn't tell exactly what he was thinking, but she had to admit that it seemed like the best solution, at least for the time being.

With everyone in agreement and with the two deputy sheriffs waiting outside, they went back into the house. "Mr. Halstrom," Denitra began, "we are obligated to take your child into shelter for the evening. She will be well cared for; I guarantee that. This is a normal practice when a child is injured, and we don't know exactly why. At this point, this is nothing personal. There will be a hearing before a judge tomorrow, and you or your wife can show up and explain things, and the judge can make some decisions then. Do you understand?"

Mr. Halstrom stood there, eyes moistening. He turned and walked out of the kitchen and reappeared with the child, Amy Jo. He stood in the kitchen doorway, saying, "You people got four armed deputies here asking for my daughter—nobody hurt her. You don't even know what happened. We don't know either. Not like we have a choice now."

His wife still hadn't moved. Her head was still down on the kitchen table.

Cameron said, "Mr. Halstrom, your child will be absolutely safe, and we'll be in touch every day until we figure this out. I promise."

Halstrom looked at Cameron and then dropped his head down to Amy Jo to kiss her and said, "You'll be back. Be brave, honey." Then he handed her over to Denitra. Amy Jo bawled all the way to the sheriff's cruiser.

Chapter 13

HOME VISITS

Cameron and John headed back to town in a car hot as blazes. She wasn't going to turn on the AC, even if it did work. "Roll down the windows," she said. "I'm saving gas."

"For real? I can hardly hear you with the wind blowing through the car. Don't run off the road. Look at that gator. *Jesus!*"

"We'll be on the main road in a second. So relax, Florida man. Can you listen and stop surveying the wildlife? That was a stressed encounter at the Halstroms'. Nothing about that feels good."

"Cam, did you see those birds? Beautiful. I love it out here: rugged but pretty. Well, kind of pretty for a swamp." John looked over at Cameron. "Yeah, I know, bad stuff. You're right, it's hard. Gives you an in-your-face idea of what a tough job the deputy sheriffs can really have, taking kids to shelter."

"I've never seen you react to birds and stuff like this," Cameron said, shaking her head with an expression of disbelief. "And anyway, since when did you decide to take charge and let the deputies take the child? I mean, I like it, you being the Man. What's going on? You go to a couple of bars and act like Joe Hunk the policeman."

"What? Joe Hunk? There's no Joe Hunk. It's Joe Friday."

Cameron ignored that. "Look, now we're on the main road. Feel better? Anyway, I know the cop Joe Friday was on TV fifty years ago; disregard the hunk stuff, loosen up, it's not that big a deal. I was just saying. Anyway, I know because I watch the History Channel. Listen, I'm not feeling well, are you? That shook me up, and I got a knot in my stomach. Is this stress or what? And all for a salary of $30,000 a year. I'm going to see a shrink. I mean literally, my friend Dr. Camp."

"Cam, I feel fine, but yes, we've a lot on our plate; I get that, and I feel out of my element too. No way to avoid it. This may sound strange, but maybe we can get a handle on Alisha Santeroa and Sandra Williams if we go do some home visits when we get back to Tampa. I came up with nothing at the bars except to get a better idea of the guy with the arrow tattoos. Which one was that anyway, Juan or Jack? I'm getting confused."

"Yeah, I know," Cameron responded. "It's the Jack guy, the one with the tattoos. You remember his so-called sister. I don't know; don't you think we've done enough digging today? I'm tired, not in the best of shape right now."

Looking out the window, wind whipping his hair into a frenzy, John complained, "Are you going to start speeding and passing cars now? Let's just drive a bit slower. This is confusing, to say the least. We're dealing with some characters, not exactly the normal stuff."

Cam said, "What do you mean, not the normal stuff? This is totally normal. I have to keep my eyes on the road. Don't get me sidetracked. Halstrom and his family are definitely normal stuff, but in our world they're not. When was the last time you had a case with a mother and a father and all otherwise healthy children? I mean, never."

"Well, the Halstroms aren't rich, but rich people can be psycho, too. We've seen them. You know what I'm talking about, Cam."

"I'm not talking about rich people. Where'd that come from? I'm talking about what looks like a normal family but in fact isn't. I agree with you: let's do some home visits. Might as well push on. It's worth a shot."

"God, Cam, get off the interstate! That guy almost sideswiped us."

"Oh my God, don't be so dramatic. What do you expect? Let's go see Alisha first. I still can't get over Judge Crowe letting Elijah go home. And then she shelters the Williams kid. Yin and yang, and it leaves me holding the bag." Cameron was on a roll.

John looked again over at Cameron, still gripping the dashboard and his door.

"Look," she said, "we're doing guesswork here. It's not like anyone gave us a manual on how to protect a kid and a family when we started this job. We got those classes on how the system works: the courts, the assistant attorneys, the tip hotline, the role of Kids Care, how the judges and bureaucrats fit together. But they never taught us who to keep in shelter, who to trust, or how to figure out when the paramour is a lying sack of shit. But we're still responsible. I mean, I'm committed to justice, and I hate child beaters, but really? All these people have hardships I don't want to have myself."

"I know; agreed," John said, praying they'd be off the interstate soon.

Cameron went on. "Take Alisha Santeroa. What do we really know about her? Nothing. Is she a liar? Something takes her from one difficult situation to another. Is she afraid of her mother? I mean, what is that all about? Or maybe she's just unlucky. Why can't she hold down a job? She doesn't show any signs of drug abuse now. That's good, but why not? I don't like it, and I can't explain it. And Judge Crowe is basically clueless except for what we tell her."

John sat there, saying nothing. Cameron slowed the car down and stopped talking. What a relief: now he could look out the window without worrying about getting killed.

He couldn't disagree with Cameron's frustrations, which mirrored his own. How was he ever going to be able to have a wife and a family with this job and its miserly salary? Sure, the retirement benefits were good, but that would be thirty or forty years of commitment at least.

But there wasn't time to think about that now. "Cam, let's deal with Alisha and Sandra. Then we can go to Sam's and unwind. Does that work for you?"

"You win. Works for me."

They arrived at Alisha's apartment around 7:00 p.m. Alisha answered the door. Elijah was in his crib, asleep. Juan Martinez was not there. Cameron asked if she and John could visit and apologized for the lack of notice. Alisha brought them into the kitchen, where they sat around a small table.

The apartment was basic and functional, and the kitchen was tidy and clean. There were colorful artificial flowers, lots of plants, and some patterned throw rugs on the linoleum floor.

Cameron told Alisha that she and John were impressed with Alisha's work on her case plan, her parenting class, and her job skills class. She had perfect attendance, and it was nice that her mother was so involved and supportive. "We wanted to reach out to get a better understanding and to lend a helping hand," Cameron said. "That's why we showed up the other day when Juan was at the apartment. We didn't know he was in the picture, and there are some concerns about him and his anger issues."

"We're hoping we can make a new start here," John added.

"I'm still pissed at you guys," Alisha said. "You took Elijah, and you put him in a shelter!" She said she knew their job was to protect Elijah, but there was no need for any protection against Juan. "He's a great guy," she insisted. "Never laid a hand on Elijah or me."

"How long have you known him?" Cameron asked.

"About two months," Alisha replied. "I met him with some friends hanging out around here one night."

"I'm glad to hear more about his background," Cameron said. "And yeah, I get it; you're upset, but we're not happy with Juan's behavior. We felt intimidated by him. He was aggressive."

Alisha stood up, placed her hands on her hips, and leaned forward. "He was in your face, thinking you were here questioning how I was raising my son. What the fuck! That's not so bad. I like his protection. Maybe he really likes me and Elijah and sticks up for me."

"Okay, I can see and respect that; no need to get mad. We come in peace. We really thought Juan was over the top—in our opinion. We were thinking of protection for you and Elijah."

Alisha was clearly still angry with them. "You guys need to back off. I'm telling you, he's good for me and Elijah. Never threatened us. What else can I say? Please. He's good."

"Okay, okay. Look, I get it. John gets it. We'll get out of here in a minute. Glad to know he's good for you and Elijah. Truthfully, that helps us, and thank you. Is there anything else we should know? Problems with money, childcare, work, anybody else, that kind of thing?"

"No," Alisha said. "I'm good now. No drugs. My mother is always around when I need her, even for some extra money. Thanks."

"Okay, later," Cameron said. She and John looked at each other, and when he had nothing to add, they left the apartment.

"Well," John remarked, "that was a bunch of nothing. Exactly what she or anyone would say. We need confirmation from others. No way can we go before Judge Crowe with nothing but speculation."

They decided to drive over to Sandra's apartment, about five minutes away. It was 7:45 p.m., still hot and muggy out.

Cameron looked at John as he got back in the hot car. "Don't start that again," she said. "I just hope that Jack guy isn't there."

"What are you worried about? You got me for protection. I'm 'the Man,'" John said, sticking his chest out and flexing his biceps, such as they were.

Cameron laughed. "You couldn't even throw a punch. I can't imagine you in a fight. Now, that Mr. Halstrom, he's a different animal."

"You're right on that score. But no thanks for the comparison. I guess you couldn't resist. I'd be the first to run. I should be looking to you for protection. Such a tough girl."

"Look, let's not get carried away. Thanks for the laugh, but let's focus."

John said, "It'll be the same routine with Sandra, you know. Lots of blah, blah, blah, and nothing to show for it."

"I know," Cameron replied. "But let's keep laying some groundwork."

"Will do. I'll follow your lead again."

Walking into the courtyard of Sandra's apartment complex, they saw Jack Wilson hanging out with some people. It was a neighborhood party on a summer evening, still plenty warm but broiling, like daytime. Sandra was not among them.

Wilson barked, "Ohhhh, lookey here, the poooliiiceee; step back."

Neither Cameron nor John said anything, heading straight up the outside stairs to Sandra's. They knocked on the door, but there was no answer, so back they went to speak with Wilson.

Paying no attention to the fact that she and John were outnumbered, Cameron said, "Where's Sandra?"

"Me? Don't know. You already took the kid." Wilson looked like his big, typical, roughneck self, with his tight-fitting jeans and muscle shirt, sweaty but not dirty.

"Do you know where Sandra might be?"

"No."

"Have you seen her today?"

"Nope. Sorry."

"You know, Mr. Wilson, we are not the cops."

"I know you hang out with cops. What's the difference?"

Gesturing toward the guy standing next to Wilson, John asked, "Who's your friend here?"

The friend said nothing, his expression conveying zero interest.

With some swagger, Wilson responded, "You saw him at the bar this morning. Striker, say hello."

Striker said nothing and walked away, literally walking out of the patio with no goodbyes or remarks.

John and Cameron walked off too. "Let's go talk to some neighbors," Cameron said.

Sandra's next-door neighbor was the one who had found David crawling around on the balcony yesterday. When they knocked on her door, she asked them to step inside. She told them that she wasn't taking care of David yesterday, and she had called the hotline.

"Thank you very much. May I have your name again?" Cameron asked.

"Delores Reed." Delores looked to be in her late sixties and for some reason wasn't afraid of the company Sandra kept. An old man was in the apartment, sitting upright in a lounge chair. He lifted his hand to say hello. He seemed impaired in some way, but it wasn't clear how.

"That's Frank, my husband," Delores said. "Fifty years. He'd get up, but a wave is good enough for him."

"Good evening, Mr. Reed," Cameron and John said in unison.

"Delores, how is Sandra today? You know David is in shelter," Cameron said.

"I know—well, I figured. She came home last night, but I haven't seen the boy. She left early this morning, I assume looking for a job. Our walls are so thin we hear everything."

Interesting, Cameron thought. "How is Sandra as a neighbor?"

"She's good. Seems like she's always away, looking for a job. We look after David."

"How often?"

"Sometimes three days a week; depends on what Sandra is doing. He's a sweet boy and likes to nap in the morning and afternoon, so I get a break. I've got a key to her apartment and use her crib. I don't know why I made the call yesterday, but it seemed like the right idea. It's not a good idea to rely just on Mr. Reed and me."

"Okay," Cameron said. "Don't worry about it. You did the best thing. Our job is to put some additional eyes on David and to help Sandra along. You understand that?"

"Yes. I do. We're always talking to Sandra. She's pretty open with us. We listen, we support her. She's a nice girl. Sometimes she's in her apartment for days without coming out, nice and quiet. A little odd, I think, but she tells us she likes it quiet. We hear David cry sometimes, but not a lot, just every so often. Then they'll be away for a few days. Mostly she comes home at night but not always."

"Does she have a lot of friends? We did see Jack Wilson downstairs."

"We don't know about her friends. We see that guy Jack sometimes."

"How about his friend Striker?"

Delores stepped out of the unit and peered over the rail, very slowly and carefully, and then stepped back inside quickly. "I don't see anyone downstairs except Jack Wilson. Wilson's a newcomer, maybe been around about a month. Sandra always has a boyfriend. She is pretty, don't you think?"

"Yes, I do."

John had yet to say anything. He stood just inside the door, expressionless but attentive, hands in back pockets. Delores didn't seem to mind.

Cameron continued. "Delores, have you had any experience with Jack Wilson, or do you have any ideas or concerns about him?"

"I see him and say hello. He's new, like I said. He's not clean—looks sweaty. These young people: tattoos and crazy clothes. We stay away from him. I like to be friendly, but I lock my door. I don't know him. I don't like him around Sandra or David, but I hear him in the apartment. He watches TV, yells and curses. He leaves in the morning, but always late, like around 11:00, when Sandra is at home. She doesn't ask him to take care of David, if that's what you want to know. You know what I mean?"

"Yes. Does he have a job that you know of?" Cameron asked.

Delores shrugged. "I don't know what he does. I'm not a busybody, you know."

"I know," Cameron said, thinking the remark funny, but politely avoiding the point.

"Do you think Wilson stays in the apartment with Sandra when she is there?" John asked.

"Maybe yes, maybe no; I'm just not sure. It gets real quiet."

Cameron said, "Thanks, Delores. We'll be back, on and off. You and Mr. Reed take care. Talk to you later." She and John left and went back to the car. There was no more they could do that night, so it was time to blow off a little steam at Sam's.

Chapter 14

SAM'S

When Cameron and John entered Sam's, it seemed as though everybody in town was there, including Nick and Daniel. John wasn't a regular, like Cameron, so he ventured off by himself after grabbing a beer. Cameron noted John's typical behavior: the standoffish routine, acting carefree but taking everything in. John wasn't ashamed of keeping his eyes on Cameron as she interacted with her friends. He watched Daniel grab her, hoist her into the air, and kiss her neck. Cameron was loving it and glanced over at Nick to ensure that he hadn't missed any of it.

"What's happening, beautiful girl?" Daniel exclaimed. "Seems like you spend all your time working these days."

"What can I say? Exhausted and happy," Cameron said. "John's keeping me alive and busy—no rest, just work, but all's good, I hope. Anyway, here we are."

Nick jumped in. "What's up?" he said, leaning in for a light, quick hug. She looked up at him with a funny-looking, squished face, pulling her eyebrows down toward her eyes and pressing her lips together in a pout. *A light hug?* she thought. That wasn't good enough. Cameron grabbed him for a long, hard hug and said, "That's better."

"Yeah, thanks. That was good," Nick said. He looked so helpless that Cameron could hardly resist. He was just too handsome to pass up, even if his hair was out of place and he needed a shave.

Daniel broke in, saying, "You know, we all should go to the beach or something this weekend. It's been a while." He smiled and said, "How about it?"

"Agreed," Cameron said happily.

Nick said, "I say we all go to a Rays game. How about that?"

John heard this invitation but hung back. He wanted to go to a Rays game too; he liked baseball. But they weren't asking him. So much for that. He wandered back over to the far end of the bar. Clearly, both Nick and Daniel were entranced by Cameron, and there was no way he could compete with that. Thank God there was a TV at the bar with a sports news program on. Left to his own thoughts, he started stressing out again about making only $33,000 a year and working around the clock. Then there was the crazy "police work" he found he wasn't able to resist. But right now, he might as well be reading case files and inputting data into FinCen.

He walked over to Cameron and said, "Sorry, guys, I'm done for the night."

"Catch you in the morning, then," Cameron said. "You okay?" She gave him a quick hug and a questioning look.

Of course he liked the hug, so he wasn't totally left out. He said he was fine and told her to stay and have a good time. He called a cab to get home. But he was mad at himself for not trying a bit harder to fit in.

Cameron thought for some reason that this was not John's night. She watched him walk out.

"He's a bit of a loner," Nick said, watching John leave.

"He's a great guy," Cameron said, feeling protective. "I guess he needs space tonight. Tough day, trust me."

"Maybe we can get him to a ball game," Daniel said. "If he's into it, I mean."

"That's a great idea! John's actually kind of a baseball freak, from what I can tell," she said.

"Fine with me," Nick said.

"Okay," she said. "Let's have a few beers and enjoy." She went over to the bar and grabbed a stool. Daniel and Nick did likewise, sitting on either side of her and hailing the bartender for some beers. They had a lively discussion. Daniel led the way, which Cameron noticed, thinking to herself, *He's always thinking about the group as a whole. Nick is a bit more solitary.*

After an hour of plans for the baseball outing, laughs about country music, and a few political snippets about Obama, the new president, Cameron called it quits. It had been a long, troublesome day, and she needed to get home.

Chapter 15

A BLANKET AND A RUG

That same night, the man named Striker showed up at both Sandra's and Alisha's apartments.

Striker, above all else, liked to stay away from police, which to him included any DCF or other government types. His practice was to bum shelter from various people—acquaintances rather than friends, if one could even say he had any—and to migrate from place to place. He hung out at bars with at least pocket change and was able to move silently under the radar. He always had some money. He never hustled anyone, and he didn't do drugs. He didn't have a job and didn't seem to owe anyone. His source of money was never clear—maybe some type of pension or government money. He might have served in the military. No one knew for sure. He seemed brazen.

He was of average height and, like Jack Wilson, lanky, apparently well fed but not muscular. He looked about forty-five and had a weathered, scraggly face. His closely shaved hair had a bit of gray. He aroused attention with his steely green eyes and big strong hands and feet.

At the bar earlier, Striker had left immediately when John Quint came in asking about Jack Wilson. He later found Wilson at the court-yard of Sandra's apartment, after meandering around Suitcase City and Thirtieth Street, popping in and out of houses, bumming a place to stay. He wasn't stupid; in fact, based on his vocabulary and awareness of current events, just the opposite. Maybe he wasn't polished, but he was well read, and he could readily put words and thoughts together, which he was happy to do at any time and place when the Man was nowhere to be found.

Even later that evening, he ended up in East Tampa near the main east–west highway of Hillsborough Avenue. A number of people crashed there that evening, mostly smoking and snorting junk, and there was some offhand sex. The toilet was in the middle of the house, exposed, free for use by anyone, irrespective of gender. Conventional rules of behavior did not apply.

Striker walked into the front yard in a high mood. He enjoyed his own conversation, and that evening there were some of his acolytes, who enjoyed his banter too.

"I saw the Man today," Striker said. "Geeky guy: collared shirt, fancy pants, walking around asking questions. He must've known he'd learn nothing. But he was asking this and that. Name was John something. Not a cop, but it doesn't matter. They're all ready to shoot us because we aren't them, whatever the fuck the color you are. I hate those motherfuckers.

"Yeah, okay, *chill out*, all of you say. You say chill out, man, relax, be cool. I say I can't take oppression and arrogance. We need to be free where we work, eat, and sleep; no fear of being beaten up or shot. You say just enjoy—the smoke, sex, whatever. I get that, man; I can go with that but can't abide by the rest. I don't owe the Man, and he doesn't own me."

He pointed at his listeners and said, "You and you, listen up. Why should I be angry? Everyone should be angry. I'm full of anger. And I'm not a fool. I'm out of here." He threw up his arms and hands, hoisted up his pants, and sauntered out of the yard and down the street.

It was around 11:00 p.m. Striker headed for Sandra Wilson's apartment. Maybe Jack would be there, and he could crash at Sandra's. At least that kid wasn't there, so there wouldn't be any crying. He'd stay out of the way of those old folks next door. Lie low and get some sleep in dry quarters.

When he got to Sandra's, Jack opened the door. "You got to get out of here, man. The old folks talked to Sandra about them speaking to a child agency. She's spooked."

"Man, you told me she was okay with this. I'm here now," Striker whispered.

"She changed her mind. Sorry, man. Now, you get." Wilson pushed his arms out, back and forth.

Striker left, creeping down the outside hall and then the metal stairs in absolute silence. He headed to Alisha Santeroa's. He could always count on her, though she could be mercurial, and she had this new straight-up boyfriend who maybe had a legit job. Striker felt that he and Alisha were like soulmates—but he knew no more than that. It was only about three or four blocks away, although she had rebuffed him the night before.

A light was on in the apartment, but he heard no voices. No sign of the boyfriend. He knocked.

Whispering through the door, Alisha said, "Striker, I told you not to call me, not to hang out around here. That bitch DCF woman, Cameron whatever, is all over me. I got to be careful. Elijah is asleep."

"Where's the Spaniard?"

"Not here."

"I need a place to stay without a bunch of freaks around me. I was at the house earlier but couldn't take it. Girl, you know that scene can be hard on me. I end up just talking shit to myself. Everyone there is stoned."

"Get in here and be quiet," Alisha said, opening the door. "You can crash, but you got to leave before Elijah wakes up."

Alisha was just out of the shower, with wet, stringy hair, blond with soft reddish streaks, almost orange in places. She was tall, with silky legs not covered by her nightclothes and strong, sleek shoulders and long arms, all visible for Striker to admire, which he did.

"Damn, Alisha, you are hot tonight."

Twisting her hair with her right hand, she said, "Shut up, big boy, and don't say another word. And stop staring at my hair."

She turned, took a step back, reared her head from the stench, and raised her hand to cover her nose. "You stink, Striker. I mean really stink. And those clothes! Go take a shower and hang up the clothes in the bathroom after you wash them. You can sleep under that blanket lying over there. Anyway, you got nothing I haven't seen before. Just stay away from me."

"Aww, don't talk like that," Striker said. "You go to sleep without me, that's fine. Hard to imagine, but I just want to sleep. You need to junk that boyfriend. He's a toy of a man, that Spaniard."

"Be quiet," Alisha said. "I'll see you early in the morning. Job hunt tomorrow."

"Oh, you're with the Man. I don't like it."

"Good night, Striker. See you in the morning. Now shut the fuck up, and don't say another word." She grabbed a towel and the blanket and threw them at Striker. "There you go," she said. "Now get in the shower."

"Yes, ma'am." He showered and crawled under the blanket on a rug, falling asleep right away. He was out of the apartment by 7:00 the next morning.

Chapter 16

HOTLINE

Cameron and John met at their office first thing the next day. They talked briefly about their three cases: the Halstroms, Alisha and Elijah Santeroa, and Sandra and David Williams. They decided John would come up with a game plan for Santeroa and Williams, and Cameron would start on the Halstrom case. They settled into their respective cubicles.

John was no novice, but standard protocols were proving useless in the Santeroa and Williams cases. The mothers were following their case plans. On the other hand, both were involved with men who, on a visceral level, didn't square with either his thinking or Cameron's.

John's fieldwork the day before wasn't standard procedure—walking into a bar in a troubled part of town and then, a couple of hours later, going into another one just outside the Twenty-Second Street Causeway. The fact that he'd done that continued to surprise him. Why was he going to such lengths? He wasn't a cop; he had no weapons, had never handled a gun, and considered himself to be a nerd.

What was motivating him? Cameron? Was he trying to go out with a bang—literally? He laughed at himself, a loud, boisterous sound, at the thought that he had an unknown personality defect, though one he felt happy about.

"What's so funny?" Cameron asked from the depths of her cubicle.

"Just thinking about what we're up to. It's crazy, real crazy. You know some good shrinks?"

"You're right, no kidding, but it is what it is," Cameron replied. "I'm just saying. Hey, were you okay last night? You should join us for a ball game. What do you say?"

The invitation surprised him. He was quick to respond. "Yeah, sure, sounds good. I'd like that. I could do some play-by-play and educate you and your friends."

"Calm down, tiger. You be nice."

"Got it. And thanks."

———

Cameron headed to court with some explaining to do in front of Judge Crowe about the little girl with a broken shoulder. She'd have to figure out a new approach so that this time the judge would agree with her.

At 9:10 a.m., Judge Crowe entered the courtroom, looking drowsy, her hair somewhat of a mess. Had she had a hard night? She got right down to business. "Madam clerk, what do we have first thing this morning?"

"Your honor, we have a temporary shelter case: a three-year-old minor, name of Amy Jo Halstrom. She is in shelter."

"Thank you," the judge said. "Who is here on this case? I see you, Ms. Springer; back again today? This is our week, isn't it?"

"Yes, your honor. Good morning, I'm on the Halstrom case,"

Cameron said with a nice, businesslike smile but thinking, *Here we go again, and I have no idea of what to say.*

"Do we have a guardian ad litem?"

"Yes, ma'am. My name is Lara Liu," said the woman. She was well dressed, in a nice khaki skirt and white blouse topped with a light-blue, tweed suit jacket. She looked like a professional and well-established young lawyer. "This is my first time in your courtroom. I'm an attorney who volunteers pro bono as guardian on occasion. I received word about this case last night, and I arranged for Mr. Chad Burt to serve pro bono as my attorney."

"Yes," Judge Crowe acknowledged, "I see Mr. Burt. Nice to see you again. This must be our week together as well. I appreciate your and Ms. Liu's service. Anybody else in this case? I see an attorney from the state is at the table."

The attorney responded, "Yes, your honor, I'm here but have no information on this case yet. I have some later hearings."

"You're here, so go ahead and lend an ear. We have another long docket today, so we might as well get going. Ms. Springer, please tell us what's going on."

"Yes, Judge. Amy Jo Halstrom is three years old. She lives with her mother, father, and three siblings. They're in a house in east Hillsborough County. The father works on a cattle ranch. Along with two investigators from the sheriff's office, and my co-caseworker and boss, John Quint, I met with Mr. and Mrs. Halstrom yesterday afternoon. DCF received a hotline tip from a hospital about Amy Jo, who was in the emergency room yesterday morning with a broken and bruised shoulder. Apparently, it appears there was some concern about possible child abuse."

Judge Crowe broke in. "Are the parents here? I see a woman at the end of the conference table. Are you Mrs. Halstrom?"

The woman stood and answered softly. She wore a simple flower-patterned shift and no makeup. Her stringy hair hung loosely around her shoulders. "I'm not the mother, but I'm a Halstrom. My brother is Amy Jo's father."

"Where are the parents?" Judge Crowe inquired.

"My brother works on a ranch and had to be at work early. He hoped to get off, but sometimes it's not easy. He's not a boss. He asked me to show up this morning. His wife, Mary, isn't feeling well. I wasn't at the house when Amy Jo broke her shoulder."

"All right, thank you, Ms. Halstrom. You may sit down. Ms. Springer, please continue. Why did you say there were apparent concerns about child abuse?"

"Judge, I said 'apparent' because someone at the hospital called the DCF hotline. In addition to the broken shoulder, there was some bruising, as reported to me by the investigator. The bruising might be indicative, but not necessarily. The three other children showed no signs of abuse. The house was not unkempt, and there was food there. No one appeared malnourished. However, the mother was not responsive, meaning she said nothing and appeared disoriented. The father didn't know how the shoulder came to be broken. The father was cooperative in the sense he spoke with us, but unable to give any explanation for the broken shoulder. The other children are ages five, seven, and nine. We did not interview them."

"How do you know the child didn't fall off a chair or suffer some other accident?" the judge asked.

"We don't," Cameron admitted.

The judge continued her questioning. "Ms. Liu or Mr. Burt, do you know anything about this case?"

"No, your honor," Ms. Liu said.

"Ms. Springer, why aren't the two investigators here?"

"Judge, we spoke yesterday, and given their schedule and my open schedule this morning, we agreed I would appear," said Cameron. "Yes, it's unusual, but I did become part of the initial investigation and removal of the child to shelter."

"All right. So, Ms. Springer, what do you want to do? The absence of the parents here is not particularly helpful, that's for sure."

"Judge," said Cameron, "we think the child should be kept in temporary shelter for a few more days so we can try to sort things out. We shouldn't disregard the initial assessment of the medical staff at the hospital. We are troubled by the mother's condition. The mother isn't well—I mean does not appear emotionally well."

"Ms. Halstrom?" Judge Crowe asked.

"Yes, ma'am," Mr. Halstrom's sister answered and again stood up.

"Ms. Halstrom, what is your first name?"

"Jane."

"What is wrong with your sister-in-law?"

"You mean Mary?" Jane Halstrom asked. She remained standing, arms by her sides as if at attention. She kept looking directly at the judge.

"Is that the first name of your brother's wife?"

"Yes. They call themselves married, but there was no formal wedding to my knowledge."

"Did they get a marriage license?"

"I don't know. I do care for the kids a lot. They're good kids, and we all take care of them good." She smiled at the judge. "We love those kids."

"Thank you, Ms. Halstrom. Does Mary Halstrom have some medical issue?"

"I don't know. She was fine, but maybe she got under the weather. I don't know nothing about it."

"All right, Ms. Halstrom, thank you. You may sit down again and relax. Appreciate your being here today. I approve the temporary shelter for now; let's have a status hearing shortly. Madam clerk, please prepare a notice. Thank you all."

Cameron sat in her chair for a moment, taking in the decision, and then nodded her head at the judge. When she left the courtroom, she thought, *Did I just communicate to the judge my approval?* She hadn't meant to do that and didn't want to give away how she felt. But the judge had approved her recommendation this time, and she left the court feeling more confident than she had before.

Chapter 17

UNDERCOVER

During the court hearing, while Cameron was addressing Judge Crowe about Amy Jo Halstrom, John was back into his cops-and-robbers routine, hitting the streets for information about Juan Martinez and Jack Wilson. At least he had AC and didn't have to drive around in Cameron's car, he thought.

He now knew that neither Jack Wilson nor Juan Martinez showed up on any serious criminal court records—just petty stuff, no felony charges or anything like that, though Juan had been on probation for a bar fight, which John thought was no big deal but was somewhat in line with Cameron's earlier concerns about Martinez. He decided to check in with the Tampa Police Department, where he had some friends and other contacts.

At police headquarters, he spent some time with an old friend, who gave him tips about connecting with the beat cops in Suitcase City, Twenty-Second Street, and Port Tampa Bay.

When he caught up with the beat cops in their cruiser, he told them about his friends at headquarters and what he was trying to do: learning facts through some fieldwork. They gave him two pieces of advice: first, don't do it.

"Second, if you're going to go ahead anyway," one cop said, "then change into some jeans, a T-shirt, and scruffy shoes, and give it a shot. Don't go around dressed like that, or no one's going to talk to you."

Of course, John thought. He should have known he wouldn't blend in, looking like his regular, clean-cut self. His car was pretty old and beat up, so he knew that wasn't a problem.

"And you should give a heads-up to the mothers involved, try to make sure Martinez and Wilson don't freak out," another cop told him. "Word on the street, in any neighborhood, spreads fast."

John thanked them and headed home, sending a text to Cameron. "Going home—got to change clothes."

When Cameron got the message, she thought it was funny—she didn't really think John was going to be able to perform miracles out there on the street, but at the same time, he was a little odd these days. She texted back: "Let's meet up at noon for lunch in Ybor City near downtown at the Tropicana Café, good Cubans and devil crabs." There they could coordinate their game plan, and she could tell him about Judge Crowe's decision that morning.

They met over Cuban sandwiches and Spanish bean soup and worked up some plans. John had stopped by a TJ Maxx to pick up a T-shirt, but he wasn't going to admit that to Cameron. They decided that John was going to see what he could pick up around town, and Cameron would go back to the office and read everything in the DCF records on Alisha and Sandra to see if there was anything they'd missed. Maybe the DCF history records would actually amount to something.

Once again, they split up. John headed to Suitcase City and Cameron back to her office and computer. She poured herself a cup of coffee and put her feet up on her desk, wishing she was wearing more comfortable shoes than the pointed-toe pair she'd worn for court. She kicked off her shoes and started to read, beginning with Alisha's case as a minor mother. Except for a few coffee breaks, she was in front of the computer for six straight hours.

By 7:30, she'd made some notes on both cases. Alisha had graduated from high school. There was one detention for smoking pot, but it was dismissed in the drug court, with the implementation of a case plan, which she'd completed. One caseworker had said she exhibited bad judgment and hung out with the wrong people. Alisha was able to work, and she liked working, but she also had a hard time holding down jobs. She'd been a waitress at a couple of fast-food places and a lawn care laborer.

Cameron thought the following case note of particular interest, written when Alisha was in high school:

> Alisha is a bright and inquisitive young lady. She is very pretty, and apparently, she has no problems with attraction of boys and maybe some young men already out of school. She would do better with her grades, in my opinion, if she were to spend more time with her studies. I think in some sense she is open with me. We have lengthy and healthy conversations, but she holds back. I can't put my finger on it, but sometimes it seems like she's playing me.

Cameron read carefully, hoping for more follow-up information, but she couldn't find any. It looked like the caseworker had either quit or was reassigned about three months after the date of the notes. *Anyway*, Cameron reminded herself, *food for thought*.

The notes on Sandra were skimpy, just as Denitra had said. Pat Smith, the caseworker on vacation, had entered notes under the case of David Williams. Sandra did not appear in the system until information on David was posted, but David was posted into the system because of Sandra's drug problem. As soon as she gave birth, she was screened as a drug addict, so the state stepped in and placed David under supervision, which became de facto supervision of Sandra. Sandra didn't fight the supervision so long as David stayed with her. Pat Smith had entered notes almost every day, even if it was a simple line that nothing happened on a given day. Sandra looked for and obtained employment but didn't hold down a job for any significant period of time. The file was negative on continued drug use, but who really knew? Sandra did clerical work, mostly at insurance agencies. She had gone to classes at the local junior college off and on. Cameron saw no information on parents or other family members. How could Sandra work and take care of David with only intermittent help from her neighbor, Delores? That didn't sound right. Possible, but far-fetched.

After her marathon review of the case files, Cameron headed back to her apartment. The car was hot as ever, even if the sun hadn't set. She waited outside the car for a few minutes with the doors open, hoping for a breeze to cool things down a little.

On her way home, after slowly simmering down, her thoughts drifted back to Alisha and Sandra, wondering whether she would think twice about them if not for their involvement with Juan Martinez and Jack Wilson.

While Cameron was at the office reviewing computer records, John had driven up to Suitcase City, parked in a strip mall, and started canvassing fast-food restaurants, gas stations, a car wash, a barbershop, a computer repair store, and a sandwich shop. He was beginning to get a better sense of life in this area: who lived there and what made it tick.

In a bar, he listened to the conversation of a bunch of loud young people. He then left and drove south, crossing the Hillsborough River and cutting over to Twenty-Second Street. By then it was after 4:00, and there were a bunch of people hanging out at an outside bar, including some day laborers, all young and drinking beer. John stood out in the crowd, despite the change to a T-shirt and jeans. Hearing nothing relevant, he left, the stares of the patrons drilling into his back. He figured the whole day had been a waste of time. Maybe his jeans were too clean and his shirt too obviously brand new.

Back at his apartment, he took a cold shower and ate an early dinner and then drove to Cameron's apartment to head over to Sam's. But he didn't find her. He called her from Sam's at about 7:45; she said she was in her car, headed home, and couldn't talk because of traffic. "I reviewed all of the case notes," she said. "I'll tell you about it tomorrow."

When she got home, Daniel called. She was happy to talk to him, and glad it wasn't John; she needed a break from work, at least for one night.

"Just thought I'd check in," Daniel said. "How are you?"

"I spent six hours poring over case notes," Cameron told him. "The caseload on three cases is crushing me right now." Cameron was sitting up in a chair, munching on potato chips and drinking a beer, which would probably be dinner for the night.

"Ugh, sorry. I'm stressed out too, busting my ass negotiating the purchase and sale of mortgages in a poor market, with the financial meltdown this year. Lots of money on the line, but not for me. I'm only a broker. And the mortgage market is a mess right now, with all the foreclosures. If I don't get to Sam's or hit the gym, I'm toast."

"At least you're making money," Cameron reminded him.

"Yeah, I'm fine with the money, but I'd like to make more."

"Me too. I'm caught up in this do-good stuff. I mean, I like it—the truth is I *really* like it. I think I'm really doing something good, maybe important even. I get little money and no gold stars. The kids are great, though." She moved over to her couch, stretched out, and put her feet on top of a pillow.

"Believe me, Cam, you're doing good."

"Unless you're taking some parent to a doctor's appointment or the drugstore, or picking up their groceries, it's a fight. The office is busy, and everyone is stressed with their cases, working away in their cubicles. And my own life is relegated to an occasional night out at Sam's. Thank God for that. I'm not sure the last time I was in the gym."

"Well, I'm here for you," Daniel said. With that, a thought flashed into Cameron's mind: *Is he asking for validation?*

Cameron said, "For sure. Thanks, that's good." She didn't want to say anything else, not wanting to give Daniel the wrong idea about how close they were.

"I think the game this weekend will be lots of fun," she went on.

There was an awkward pause, and then Daniel said, "Cam, you should tell me about your cases. I know they're private, but, you know, anonymously. Maybe make you feel better."

"Maybe," she said. "I appreciate that; you know I do. I feel like I've talked your ear off about it enough already, though. Look, I'm dozing off. Can we talk more tomorrow?"

"Sure," Daniel said. "Talk to you later."

Then Cameron called Grace. She had not spoken to Grace since their visit at Sam's two nights before.

"Isn't 9:00 p.m. past your bedtime?" Grace said when she picked up.

"You're the one usually asleep by now," Cameron said. "Right? Your beauty sleep, you dainty Southern girl."

"No," Grace said, "you got that backward. I'm from the backwoods, not the fancy up-east."

Cameron laughed. "New Jersey, 'the fancy up-east.' That's funny. Anyway, Daniel just called me, and he said, quote, 'I'm here for you.'"

"That's sweet," Grace said. "I mean, he likes you. You get that, don't you?"

"I don't want to lose a good friend," Cameron said. "I don't need someone in love with me now."

"Why not?"

"Come on. You know what I mean."

Grace sighed. "It's not like you're leading him on, so relax. Take it for what it is. It's not like he said he was coming over to your place with a bottle of wine or something."

"All right, I get it," Cameron said. "Thanks." They talked for another ten minutes or so, nothing specific, just checking in with each other. Finally, Cameron said she didn't have the energy to stay on the line anymore and would talk more later.

After hanging up with Grace, Cameron crawled into bed. After thirty minutes of tossing and turning, she pushed herself out of bed and went to her desk. She opened the folder containing the notes she'd taken on both cases. As she did, the phone rang. It was John.

"Hello, John," she groaned. "Why are you calling me so late?"

"Nice greeting," he responded. "It's only 10:00."

Cameron sighed. "I'm at my computer right now, looking over notes," she admitted.

"I got nowhere today," John told her. "I did the walk around Suitcase City and nothing, really nothing. But I got a feeling of what's going on there. You can tell it's a stretch every day for anyone there. You can spot the guys pushing the bad stuff."

"Maybe you should be a beat cop."

"Ha ha, I get your point. Not really funny right now," John said.

Cameron thought maybe John was actually acting a bit out of

character; he seemed actually a little sensitive, at least about the Joe Friday stuff. She decided to be careful for the moment, making sure she was being understanding and nice.

"Sorry, John, that was not called for. I just got off the phone with Daniel, and all I could do was bitch about work. Now I'm feeling guilty."

"Well, it is what it is, and it's not going to kill us. Apology accepted, and don't worry about Daniel; he is a big boy," John said.

"Okay, will do. Look, John, let's not give up just yet. I know this beat cop stuff is out of character for you, but those people know stuff. I don't know what, and I don't know how long it will take for you to find out more, but I know I don't want to be back in front of the judge without some good hard facts."

"Yeah, I'm thinking the same thing."

"Maybe Alisha needs to move back home with her mother," Cameron went on. "It might work. I need something on Juan Martinez to feel comfortable; that's my instinct. Sandra is another story. She's looking to lose custody of David if whatever's going on continues like this."

Cameron was now having a hard time getting the words out. Her eyes were watery, and she was slumped down over the phone. "I'm hurting on this, John, really hurting."

Quiet at first, John said firmly but softly, "Cam, I know it hurts. You know I care for you, really care, and you're not alone. Look, just stay on the phone a minute or two. Don't say anything, just hang out for a minute or two. Then we can maybe get some sleep."

After a while, Cameron asked, "John, are you there?"

"Yes, here," he said.

"Thanks. I think I can sleep now." Her tone was soft, and she didn't say more.

"Good night, Cam. See you tomorrow."

Falling asleep, he realized that he felt . . . good. He hoped she did too.

Chapter 18

LATE-NIGHT CALL

John's phone rang at 2:00 a.m. "Mr. Quint?" a woman's voice said. "Yes, this is John Quint." He sat up in bed, becoming alert.

"It's Delores Reed. I need to talk to you."

"Yes, Mrs. Reed. It's late, but I have time. Talk to me, please."

"Mr. Quint, Sandra's hurt, I think. Something bad is going on. I know you're not the police. There's a lot of screaming and banging next door. I don't want to get Sandra in trouble. I don't know where David is."

"I'll come over right away," John said. He was wide awake now.

"Yes, sir," she said. "Please hurry."

John called the police and arranged to meet a cruiser in fifteen minutes at Sandra's apartment. He called the beat cops he'd met earlier to request that there be no sirens. They seemed to be always on call. He thought about calling Cameron, but there was no time.

Once he arrived at the apartment complex, he gave the two police officers as much detail as he had. He went with the police to the Reeds' place. Delores opened the door cautiously, and they stepped into her apartment. She repeated to them what she had told John.

Next, they knocked on Sandra's door. It was quiet. They knocked again. Then they heard a metallic slam and a "fuck." The police broke the door in and focused their flashlights. No one appeared. The back window over the table in the dinette kitchen was open. One of the policemen looked out; coming up behind him, John looked too and saw a dumpster directly beneath the window, about ten feet down. When they went into the bedroom, they found Sandra slumped in a corner, naked and beaten up. *So this is what it feels like,* John thought to himself. He'd gone way beyond the regular duties of his job by now.

Chapter 19

CAFÉ CON LECHE

Cameron arrived in the office at 7:00 a.m. John was already there, having arrived at 4:00, directly from the hospital. When he had left, Sandra had been sedated. He gave Cameron a full report.

The police were now looking for two males, one fitting the description of Jack Wilson and the other fitting the description of Striker. John described both. He gave a good description of Wilson, given the blue and purple arrow and flower tattoos on his arms. John knew little of Striker. At least he recalled his name. Maybe it would lead to useful information.

Cameron and John shared their relief that David was in temporary shelter. Under the circumstances, that wasn't about to change anytime soon.

Almost immediately, Cameron recalled her earlier recommendation that Judge Crowe release David back to Sandra. Thank God the judge had kept David in shelter, she thought. It was apparent to her that the judge had better intuition than she did. She felt shaken. How close she had come to disaster!

John left Cameron alone for a few minutes to let her absorb the news. Then he poked his head around the cubicle. In a soft voice, he said, "Cam, you think maybe we can keep going today? Lots on the calendar. Your decision."

She looked up and stared at him for a minute. "I get it," she said. "This is hard, I mean really hard, but you know me: I'll push on. Maybe it's time to figure out housing for Sandra in some other location."

"That'll take some time, but it's not an issue right now. No telling how long Sandra will be in the hospital," John said. "That takes some pressure off. Today we'll deal with Alisha and Elijah and the Halstroms. Judge Crowe will want an update on the Halstroms tomorrow."

Cameron said, "I feel like shit. What am I doing here? I'm getting a sinking feeling that I'm in over my head."

"Believe me, Cameron, you're not in over your head. You've done this, and you can do this."

"I've just never had to deal with this kind of trauma. I don't think I know what's really going on. What am I missing? I mean, I've had some breakups with boyfriends—two, to be exact. I've always had close friends to back me up, and I have sisters and a brother. I still live under the cloud of one of the breakups. I mean, I'm not a totally innocent person here."

Pulling his chair around the cubicle, John looked at Cameron. They were both quiet for a minute. Then he leaned back and interlaced his fingers behind his head and said, "Look . . . let's take one step at a time. It's probably better if we keep working, if you think you can handle it."

"I just need to settle down a bit. I can at least go to the risk meeting this afternoon. That won't be too bad. Just give me some time to sit here, try to pull it together."

John nodded and pulled his chair back around to his cubicle.

Cameron knew she would have to deal with the risk committee meeting, and Halstrom was bound to come up. After about fifteen minutes, she and John spoke again. They decided that he would continue his quest for information on Alisha and Elijah, get back on the streets, and maybe meet someone who knew Martinez, Wilson, or Striker. Cameron would head over to the meeting.

Then Cameron spoke up. "There's something about me you don't know—and it's pretty fundamental to me and this job. I'm surprised I've never told you before, after three years working together." Her eyes watered, and her speech was halting. She stopped and looked at him, lips quivering. John was quiet and attentive.

"My sister is disabled. She got sick and just never totally recovered. It was some kind of virus. She was in the hospital for months. This is my little sister. I sat with her almost every day. I love her so much and still miss her. She's okay, basically, but her life is hard. We've all pitched in to help, and it's worked, but only to a degree. Now I'm alone down here, trying to do something good. That's a pretty big soft spot. I feel so sad and helpless sometimes, even if I'm tough on the outside."

John reached for her hands and squeezed them. "You'll be okay. Just hang here until you need to go to the risk committee meeting. Okay?"

"Yes. Love you for listening."

"No problem. But look—before I go, I need to tell you a little bit more about Judge Crowe. I've heard a lot about her over the years. She's famous for working late; everyone knows that. Four years ago, there was this case with four kids. The mother was hard into meth and hadn't been around in a while. The sheriff's investigation team removed the kids on the day of the DCF report. They were in residential care for a while but then were moved to parents of the father. Judge Crowe's one condition was that a restraining order bar the father from being with the kids under any circumstance except at a monitored visitation DCF facility. Turned out the father was good about visitation but bad about the restraining order. He had drinks at a bar and ended up at his parents' house. Apparently, the parents let him stay in the house with the kids there, in violation of the restraining order. The one-year-old was sick—crying and wouldn't stop—and the father couldn't sleep. He grabbed the child and went outside, where he fell and passed out on top of the child, who suffocated."

Cameron gasped.

John went on. "I think Judge Crowe feels this case in her gut. The father was jailed and charged with involuntary manslaughter. But the local paper went after the judge, basically accusing her and the case-worker of poor judgment and bad decisions. DCF found fault with the caseworker, and an internal investigation revealed that he was late in submitting case reports. His final report on that family wasn't in FinCen on time, so it hadn't been available to Judge Crowe at the last status hearing. The caseworker had raised questions in the report about the suitability of the grandparents, worried about their ability to control their son, and expressed doubts about the efficacy of the restraining order. At the status hearing, the caseworker raised concerns about the grandparents, but Judge Crowe went with them anyway."

John watched Cameron's face to see how she was taking it all in. "So what I'm saying, Cam, is that all of us are in the middle of it. There's lots of ambiguity, a lot of judgment calls—some good, some bad—and some disasters. You understand?"

Cameron, listening carefully, said, "Thanks. I'm not going to quit on you."

"Good. I'll see you later." John stood up to head out.

This time he went to a different café on Twenty-Second Street, fig-uring he needed to try one more time to get inside information on Juan

Martinez. He got there at 10:30 a.m. and ordered a Tampa breakfast staple: café con leche and buttered Cuban toast. The toast was warm and crispy, and the leche instantly began to perk him up.

He'd brought a newspaper with him and a paperback on guns and ammo, which he hoped might serve as cover. What he really wanted to read was the latest edition of *Psychology Today*, but that would have been a dead giveaway. He felt stressed and out of his depth. But he wasn't going to quit now, with so much at stake.

And he couldn't get Cameron out of his mind. He knew he was falling for her, but he instinctively felt he'd better keep his distance.

He ordered another leche, not able to resist the buzz and energy of the caffeine. He picked up the paper and rushed through the local news and editorials, saving the sports section for last. He read every baseball article, particularly those about the upcoming Rays game: who was in first place, recent scores, strikeouts, home runs, and triple hits, beanballs, and brawls. An hour crept by while he read and strained to listen in on any conversations in the cramped quarters of the café.

He overheard how a mechanic had jerry-rigged an overhead crane pulley, how some new containers hit the docks and how much work it meant, what a good time to leave Saturday morning for flats fishing in the bay was, someone preaching about God and his own righteousness, and finally one guy saying how he'd pulled his teenage daughter out of a drug house on Twenty-Second Street. It was the last piece that piqued John's interest.

The caffeine took hold and emboldened him. He slid off his stool and walked over to the table. "Guys, sorry, but I couldn't help overhearing your conversation about the house on Twenty-Second Street. I'm trying to protect some young people; that's my job. Do you mind if I sit down?"

The father of the teenage girl spoke up. "Well, I don't blame you for listening. Who are you?" He was in his forties and looked like it, with a big torso. His long-sleeved shirt sported the words "Tampa Steel." Not an office guy, judging by the steel-toed work boots he had on.

"I work with the Florida Department of Children and Families, for a childcare agency under the state's charge. I'm looking for some tips and information. You guys work on the docks?"

"No," the father answered. "We work with steel, just down the street, and we like Cuban food, so here we are. Don't want to get involved."

"I get that. That's all right, thanks," John said. "But maybe you can tell me where this house is, that's all."

The father gave him the location and John left, saying, "Thanks, appreciate it."

"Good luck, man."

Maybe this is something, John thought. *Am I getting the hang of this?* Before he could talk himself out of it, he went to the address the man had given him and knocked on the door. No one answered. He walked around to the back, where a lanky-looking man sat under a shade tree in a rusted metal chair, dressed in low-hanging, beat-up jeans and a dirty T-shirt and no shoes. The man said, "What's happening, my brother?"

"I'm looking around, trying to find somebody," John said. "Anybody live here?"

"Not really. Do you know me?"

"No. But I need some help."

"That so? Sorry. I'm leaving. I've seen you. You're a cop or something. That's not my business." He got up and wandered off, saying nothing more.

John figured he'd better not stretch his luck. He got in his car and turned on the AC, thanking God for that, and headed back to the office. *Sanity has prevailed*, he thought.

———

While John was in the café and poking around a backyard, Cameron had managed to pull herself together. She was still feeling unsure, but she drove to the small conference room at DCF on north Florida Avenue, not far from Suitcase City. The place was in an old strip mall with discount stores.

The people on the committee were involved in many cases. An older woman, Susan, was in charge, opening the meeting with a quick overview and concluding that little was known about the Halstroms other than that the daughter had a broken collarbone, the mother seemed unresponsive, and the father was a cowboy.

"The girl is currently safe in temporary custody," Susan said. "Of course, we can't just leave her there. We have to come up with a case plan. And what about the other three children? What are the risks, Cameron?"

"I don't know for sure," Cameron responded. "We're working on it. When we were there the family seemed okay, except for the mother. We didn't think there was any probable cause for dependency at that time, obviously, or we would have sheltered all four kids. The girl had the broken bone and was the subject of the alert from the hospital."

Susan frowned. "Yes, I can see that, but if one child is at risk, aren't the others as well?"

Steve, who was in charge of quality control and oversight within Kids Care and had years of experience with foster care systems, spoke up. "We've got to have an affirmative assessment one way or the other. If we don't and someone gets hurt, we'll all be in a deep hole. At a minimum, we'd better have some day-to-day monitoring. That's basic. Do we all agree with that?"

All agreed.

"I don't doubt any of that," Cameron said, "but temporary shelter and then foster care is a rough road. We all know that. I want to be careful. The last thing I want is an injury or, God forbid, a death, and we all know really bad stuff happens when you think you've done your best. I don't have a bad feeling about this one, but I think we should spend the time and the diligence." She was feeling a bit better—not cocky but focused enough to function and offer her perspective.

"What are your recommendations then?"

"To tell you the truth, I was hoping for a little more dialogue and maybe some other case stories to guide us. What if we up our visits and monitor heavily?"

"Great. I like that. We're in agreement on that," Steve said.

Susan spoke up. "I assume nothing came up in any of our databases or searches: no criminal activity, no arrests, no neighbor complaints, house is relatively clean? What about the father's sister? Do you think we could work harder with her, get more information?"

"Yes, the father's sister, Jane, was at the hearing. I got the impression in court she watches these kids on a regular basis. There was a guardian ad litem at the hearing: an attorney named Lara Liu. What if we solicit some help from Ms. Liu and go see the sister together? We might get some information, and Ms. Liu could pitch in."

Steve remarked, "Interesting idea; that would be novel. I have no problem with people trying to help through the guardian program; they're volunteers and can be useful, but it's not a full-time commitment. I don't care if you get her involved, but you can't shift any real responsibility to her."

Cameron was annoyed at his response. "Look, you asked me for my ideas, and she seems pretty sharp. Who knows? I'll give her a call. And find the sister, Jane."

"Okay," Susan said. "We have a plan. But we need to follow through."

After the meeting, Cameron decided that the first order of business was to contact Lara Liu, and then she would head to east county and run down Jane Halstrom.

Chapter 20

ASLEEP

Cameron got to her car, which, as usual, was hot as blazes. Saving money over having air-conditioning was a pain. She opened the car door and waited. *You're moving too fast*, she thought. *Sandra's in the hospital, David's lucky to be alive, and you're doing your usual thing: pushing forward, not taking care of yourself . . . so stop, take a minute.* She went for a short walk, sat down in the shade, and tried to settle down. How did she feel about herself and her work? Reaching deep inside, she confirmed that she actually liked herself. She was thankful for her life, for her sisters and brother. Sandra would be okay, and her kid, David, too. Somehow.

Following the decision made at the risk meeting, she called Lara Liu.

"Do you have a few minutes?" she asked when the attorney picked up.

"To tell you the truth, I'm surprised I picked up the phone," Lara replied. "I'm swamped. Billable hours, you know?" Cameron didn't know, but she made a sound of agreement. "On the other hand, I know this case is important. You want to drop by? You can come to my office downtown."

"Sure," Cameron said. "I should be there in about thirty minutes with traffic."

Once on the thirty-fifth floor of Lara's swanky office building, Cameron felt sweaty and out of place. Cool and professional Lara Liu met her at the elevator, and they went to what appeared to be a large meeting room overlooking Tampa Bay. Cameron had never seen this view except from the window of an airplane and was duly impressed by the sweeping vista of water and sunshine.

Cameron didn't waste time getting to the point. "Would you consider jumping into this case with me?" she asked Lara. "I could use the help. I know this is pretty unusual and you're obviously busy, but I just had to ask."

Lara smiled, looking humbled and surprised. She asked a few basic questions. They walked into a side room with a gleaming marble table and a beautiful and expansive view across the bay toward a long, elegant bridge. "Is that the Sunshine Skyway?" Cameron asked. Lara nodded. Beyond it lay the Gulf of Mexico.

"Wow, how do you possibly work here? This is paradise! I love it. What's this marble table for?" Cameron knew she probably sounded overly impressed, but she couldn't help it. Lara's office was so different from where she toiled every day.

"Conferences, meetings. You know. It's functional," Lara said, smiling. She motioned for Cameron to have a seat. They sat opposite each other, with Cameron looking out the window at the clear blue sky.

They got down to business. "I'm glad you called, Cameron. This is a privilege. You think I could help out? You know I'm not a child welfare expert. I've covered a few child dependency cases in court, but I've never been in the field. I spend virtually all of my time here. Sometimes

I actually sleep here between billable hours, believe it or not. But I'm interested. I mean I did sign up for the guardian program, after all. I could work with you this afternoon. People will assume I'm off visiting with a client or something."

"That would be great!" Cameron said, trying to hide her disbelief. After her boldness in reaching out to this young, smart, well-heeled lawyer, she was still surprised that she was agreeing to help.

"Just know that I haven't fully committed to anything yet," Lara said. "This is very much unknown territory for me. Okay?"

"Sure." Cameron gulped. "By the way, do you mind driving? My car is a junk heap—no AC."

Lara looked a bit surprised. "Oh. Okay. Sure. My car's in the parking garage." It was 3:00 p.m., and the two young women headed down from the thirty-fifth floor together.

Chapter 21

THE COWBOY

Cameron was enthralled with Lara Liu. In the marble and polished wood of Lara's law firm, and now in the presence of this accomplished young woman in the big money world of corporations and real estate, she felt she was in the midst of something different and exciting. Her own audacity amazed her. She wanted to make a good impression.

"Do you live in the city?" Lara asked as they drove out of the city.

"Yes," said Cameron, who was duly impressed with Lara's car. It smelled brand new, had leather seats, and was quiet. The engine didn't rumble. "I'm in West Tampa. What about you?"

"I'm not too far from downtown, in an apartment. It's fun, but I still drive to work. I know people who live downtown and hardly use their cars." Lara glanced over at Cameron, who was rubbing the leather seat. Lara smiled.

"I don't even have a car with working AC," Cameron said, adding a laugh. "And I drive a lot. I've got to have my car during the day, with court, picking up kids, interviewing relatives. All kinds of stuff. It's all interesting, but it can be a lot of work."

"Anything can be a drag," Lara said. "There's lots of pressure in my job to bring in the bucks. But I like the people. They're good. Really." She smiled and looked at Cameron. "But not too good, if you know what I mean. They're still bossy."

Cameron laughed. "Do you have to wear a suit every day?"

"Mostly."

"I only have to dress decently for court. In some ways I like it. Still, it gets hot and stuffy in the courthouse. It can feel like my car."

"You can't get out of the heat, even in the courthouse." Lara laughed. "You'd think it would be a cool place, with everything going on. Maybe stupid to say."

"No, I get it," Cameron remarked. Then she asked, "Do you like practicing law?"

"I do," Lara said.

"Do you work mostly with men?"

"Mostly, though there are women around. Women tend to do better in law school and college. It's a wonder why there are still more male lawyers in the workplace. I can't figure that out quite yet. The big issue is really why more women aren't equal in terms of making partner."

"It's just the opposite in my field," Cameron said. "At least for caseworkers like me. But at the top, it's mostly men." The two young women shared a smile.

By now they were far along the crosstown expressway headed east to the countryside. Cameron gave directions.

"I should tell you more about what I think we should do here," Cameron said, realizing she needed to focus on the work at hand. "No one knows we're coming. The idea is to show up and get some information without anyone there having time to prepare. The three boys will most likely be home from school, so that's good. I'm not sure if the father—the cowboy—will be there or not."

"A cowboy in Florida," Lara said. "Really?"

"It's not that weird," Cameron said. "Florida's a big cow state. There's lots of cowboys, even some who ride horses. They can be rough around the edges for sure, but you can usually rely on them. I've had only one case where the cowboy was a jerk, a liar, and a beater. They do like to drink."

Lara just shook her head. Clearly, she was a city girl. This was all new to her.

"Okay," Cameron said as they got closer. "So the basics are that Amy Jo is three years old. She lives with her mother, Mary Halstrom, her father, Charles, I believe, and three brothers aged five to nine. You know that from the hearing with Judge Crowe. We suspect the girl fell in some way or was hit, maybe pushed. Hospital personnel notified the DCF hotline. I think the judge left her in temporary custody because of that. Otherwise, we really didn't have anything. Judges can go one way in one case and then the other in a very similar case. I struggle with it, but what can you do?"

Lara said, "Well, lawyers and judges aren't right all the time. I have little experience in court and wouldn't know how to try a case. I'm a real estate and corporate transaction lawyer. I just put deals together; I'm never really in court. I hear about it sometimes within the firm gossip and office talk, but don't do it. The fact that you speak up and have influence in a courtroom without any legal training, that's something."

"Funny, I never thought of it that way," Cameron said. "I guess that's right, but I leave the legal mumbo jumbo to judges and lawyers, although, in my experience, I don't think the lawyers bring that much to the table. They don't really have time to learn the facts, the attorneys for the state."

"Listen to you, boss talking; you sound like a lawyer," Lara said.

"That's hilarious," Cameron said. "But seriously—I really appreciate your help."

"I'm excited about it."

"I bet Jane Halstrom, the cowboy's sister, knows plenty. Maybe she'll be at the house. If we can, we should split up: I take the mother or father, depending, and you take the sister, or we can do the reverse. Your thoughts?"

"I'll do whatever you say," Lara said. "I'm not the boss." She smiled again, and Cameron liked that she was feeling comfortable with this impressive, young woman. Maybe they had more in common than she realized.

The landscape was stark, with fields alternating with row after row of tomato plants and scrub forests where orange groves had once prospered. Cameron and Lara eventually turned right off the two-lane highway onto another asphalt road, which ran for about a quarter mile before becoming a sandy drive. Palmettos and scrub oaks lined the approach to the Halstrom house, which seemed to sink into a low-lying open area beside a cypress slough dotted with alligators.

At the house they noticed the three boys roughhousing in a side yard with a ball and bat, wrestling each other to the ground. Cameron knocked on the door, and Mary Halstrom opened it. She didn't say anything and was sullen and hunched over. They followed her into the kitchen, where the father and his sister, Jane, were sitting at a small dinette table. The mother sat and stared down. Jane said hello and invited them to sit. Her brother stood and offered his chair. Cameron thanked him. It seemed to be a good start. Lara remained standing, explaining that she sat all day.

"Thanks," Cameron said. "The first thing I want you to know, as I said before, is that I'm not the police. I have one job only, to look after

Amy Jo, and that means my hope is to reunite you with your child. That's always my hope, and I hope you can come to trust me. Jane, you met Lara in the courtroom earlier, and she's agreed to help me. She's what we call a *guardian*."

"I think I can say that you're welcome to be here at any time," Jane said. "We're friendly people, trying to do the right thing. Not sure that judge knows that. At least, I guess, you're here to learn."

"Thank you for that," said Cameron.

"You're welcome. You and the sheriff took our Amy Jo. That was wrong, just so you know. But, like I said, you're welcome here to learn the truth."

"Ms. Halstrom, please give us a chance. I understand you, but we're not bad people. I know this is awfully formal, and I apologize for that. We have a hearing tomorrow morning with Judge Crowe, so I want to get a better idea of what's going on. Do you have any questions for Lara and me?"

Mr. Halstrom turned and abruptly walked outside without saying a word. Mary Halstrom remained at the table, also silent. Cameron asked Jane if she wanted to go outside and speak with her brother.

Jane replied, "He's a big man and proud, but he can be gentle. He's very upset and he's terrified of you. Best for you to be honest with him."

"That's not good—the terrified part—but thank you," Cameron said. "I think Lara would like to speak with the two of you, if you don't mind."

"That'll be fine."

Outside, Cameron said, "Mr. Halstrom, I'm sorry, but I do need to speak with you. Please understand this is hard for me too."

He stopped but did not turn around. They both stood in silence until finally Cameron turned back to the house.

"I know you're moving. I don't see you, but I know you're moving,"

Mr. Halstrom stated in a calm, firm voice. It didn't sound like the man she had spoken with earlier in the week. She stopped and swung around.

"Yes, sir," she replied. "I was walking back to the house, but I would rather stay here and talk with you. I know you're aware I know very little. On the other hand, I expect you know more than me. Am I right about that?"

"No."

"Okay. I guess I'm wrong about that."

"I guess that depends on what you want to know, Miss Springer."

"Okay," said Cameron, at a loss. Mr. Halstrom then turned around and faced her. He stood tall, hands by his sides, motionless, like an animal about to pounce.

"Maybe I'll just go," Cameron said. "Sorry for the interruption." She wasn't quite sure what she should do and wondered how Lara was getting along with the two women inside.

"No, you're here. At least finish your business."

"Are you sure?" Cameron asked. "I can just get Lara and leave." She was feeling nervous. Maybe this had been a mistake.

"I'll tell you what, Miss Springer: you must be crazy to come over here after taking our Amy Jo with no cause. Who are you anyway? Maybe you need to explain yourself."

"Mr. Halstrom, I will do that. Is that what you want?"

He didn't move, so she began to explain herself. "Mr. Halstrom, I've been working at this job for three years. I've seen a lot of situations. Most of my cases involve what is called *family care*, where children are placed with other family members. Most of my cases involve family supervision, not taking kids away from their homes. I'm for kids staying in their homes. I want to be up front with you about that, but I also have to say that it doesn't always work that way. I don't know what really happened here with Amy Jo. I mean this in a helpful way: you should help me. I need information to help you."

Mr. Halstrom said, "You know, I still think you're the government. I don't think much of government."

"I understand," Cameron said. "Let me push you a little here, though. I can't help unless you listen and try to be patient with me. Because maybe you have helpful information and don't even realize it."

A few hours earlier, she'd been breaking down in front of John, and now she was asserting herself with a strange man in the countryside, with alligators nearby. She told herself to take it step-by-step, slow and easy.

"I'm still standing here," he said finally.

"Okay, good," said Cameron, taking a breath to steady herself. "Have you, your wife, or your sister ever hit any of the children? I don't mean a spanking but, you know, in an aggressive, mean kind of way?"

"Honestly," he said, "I don't think so, but the spanking happened. I grew up that way, and I believe in it. I know some people think differently in today's world. I'm not one of 'em."

"I get that. No problem. That was my raising too. How about the boys? Have you seen them get out of line?"

The man shrugged. "They fight. They wrestle, hit, and scream at each other. Nothing wrong with that."

"Any broken bones?"

"Been a couple with the boys—playing ball, tripping in the woods, and on the ranch falling off horses, wrestling yearlings."

"Yearlings?"

"Young calves."

"Broken bones in the house?"

"No. They're good kids, real good kids. They look after each other and after their little sister. I'm proud of the boys."

"Well, I have to ask questions." She walked toward the house and then stopped and turned to face Halstrom again. "You know I have to ask questions. I don't want to appear mean."

"So why don't you ask some better ones? Sounds as if you're looking to poke a stick at my boys. Why don't you ask me how the accident happened?"

"How did it happen?"

"I already told you; I don't know."

"Yes, I know that. That's why I didn't ask you that," Cameron said sheepishly but staring at him directly. "You're not giving me a chance." When he didn't respond, she tried another tack. "Okay, may I ask about your wife, Mary?"

"That's fine," he said. "I know she needs some help or something. She hasn't spoken but a few words to me over the last weeks, and I'm not sure what's going on. It's like she's on drugs or something."

"I'm sorry to hear that. Maybe we can look into that. She ever had a history of drugs?"

"No. She's never done wrong. Always a good Christian woman, heart and soul, and I'd know for sure. There's plenty of that stuff around. Haven't seen any in my house or on my property. I'd never allow it."

"That's good to hear," Cameron said.

"Mind you, she knows about meth," the man went on. "Seen and heard enough around here."

"Do you have any suspicion or speculation as to what happened to your wife?"

"She can be moody. She's getting older, not a teenager anymore. Maybe she's depressed. Thank God for my sister, 'cause Mary's in a different world. I keep thinking she'll snap out of it. I never hit her, if that's what you're thinking."

"No, I wasn't thinking that," Cameron said. "Well, that's all for right now. I need to speak with Ms. Liu and get ready for court tomorrow. I hope you'll be there?"

"Yes, Jane and I will be there." He looked over at the house. "Better in there," he said, walking inside.

Cameron followed. Lara, together with Mary and Jane, was seated at the dinette table. Only Lara and Jane were talking. Cameron nodded at Lara and said, "I think it's time to go. All okay in here?" Jane and Lara both nodded yes. "Okay then," Cameron said. "Let's go." Looking at the Halstroms, Cameron said, "Thanks to you, that was a helpful visit. I hope the rest of your day is good."

Lara said, "Yes, Jane, a good visit. Thanks. Bye, Mary, hope you feel better."

Cameron and Lara walked out into the yard toward Lara's car. "That was tough," Cameron said, once they were in the car. "Sorry."

"Sorry about what?" Lara asked.

"Not an easy afternoon. The cowboy—he's not college educated, that's for sure. Very country, but obviously not ignorant. How did it go for you?"

"Jane is country too. I don't know about the mother, but probably the same. She never said one word and kept her head facing down the whole time, as if something's wrong with her back." Lara seemed relieved to be in the car. She took hold of the steering wheel with two hands, pulled herself forward and down toward the wheel, and uttered, "Wow, that was something!" Sitting back up, she started the car and drove from the house, past a few alligators. Her eyes were on the dirt road. After a second, she said, "You know, Cameron, that was good. I feel good about it. Jane was very talkative."

"Really?" Cameron interjected. "The cowboy hardly has a tongue."

"She told me her whole life story, or at least it seemed like it. She's interesting. She said she and her brother grew up in the backwoods of central Florida, between a place called Wauchula and another called Belle Glade, somewhere near the Everglades."

"Interesting," Cameron said.

Lara went on. "They fished, hunted, trekked through forests, canoed down backwater creeks, and apparently spent weeks at a time in the Everglades. They knew some Indians, the Seminoles. They graduated high school, never attended college, led the life they loved. It's obvious she loves it even though she has little, if any, money. The cowboy doesn't have any either. Maybe he's one of those guys who loves the outdoors, lives poor but sits on a ton of gold. At one point, she told a story of how she and her brother were on the trail for a few weeks and ended up in a patch of palmettos and shot and killed five rattlesnakes. Look, I know I'm a neophyte, but so far nothing is obvious or makes sense here. Not sure how much that helps, but anyway, there you have it."

Lara drove and for a while neither said anything. "That was great work, Lara," Cameron finally said. "All great background stuff. Maybe the cowboy is no fraud. I just don't know."

Chapter 22

AN ENCOUNTER

As Cameron rode with Lara back to the city, she called John. "Hello," he answered, sounding sluggish.

Cameron laughed. "Did I wake you up?"

"God, I was sound asleep," he said. "Head on my desk. Sorry. Where are you?"

"In a car coming back from a meeting at the Halstroms' house. I'm with Lara Liu. Remember, I told you about her; she's the guardian ad litem. She was a big help. And there's AC in her car!"

"That's great," John said.

"Listen," Cameron continued, "Lara and I are coming up with some stuff that I think we can use with Judge Crowe tomorrow morning. It'll be dicey, but it's always dicey in that courtroom. Maybe that cowboy and the whole family aren't to blame. I don't know for sure, but maybe we have something to work with."

"That's a lot of maybes, and just a smidgen of Pollyanna thinking, but I'm all ears," John said. "Maybe I'm giddy. Anyway, I'm getting back to reality now. How about a quick dinner tonight and we talk? In the meantime, I'll head over to the hospital, check on Sandra Williams."

"Forget dinner. Go see Sandra and meet me early in the morning. I could use some quiet time tonight." Cameron hung up before John could say anything else.

John leaned back in his chair, stretched, and scratched the back of his head with both hands. Then he got up, walked to the coffee stand, poured a hot black brew, and returned to his desk. Pulling himself together, he stuffed his phone in his pocket and left for the hospital.

On his way to Sandra's room, he ran into the two beat cops from the neighborhood. It turned out they'd been assigned to the Sandra Williams matter. John asked if they had seen her. Was she lucid, and did they get any information? No, he was told; her answers were cryptic to nonexistent. The doctors said she'd woken up earlier that afternoon but recalled nothing about the beating. When they left, she was asleep again. John thanked them, asked to be kept in the loop, and told them that Sandra's kid, David, was still in shelter.

He felt restless with no Cameron to talk to, and he certainly wasn't going over to Sam's just to sit in the corner of a bar—or risk running into Daniel and Nick. He left the hospital and drove to Suitcase City, parking at the same bar where he'd encountered Jack Wilson. He assumed the cops had no workable leads on Wilson, and though he still felt out of his element, he figured he'd give it a shot. He didn't have to wait long. It was later in the evening now, and the sun was setting.

Within a few minutes, the same lanky guy from the Twenty-Second Street drug house walked down the street. John climbed out of his car and followed, his stomach turning into a big knot. The guy turned left and headed toward some apartment buildings. Sandra's building was only three blocks away. John followed, trying to stay no more and no less than a block behind, so the guy was often out of sight. Taking the same left, John spotted him again a block away, heading straight. At the next block, the guy took a right in the direction of Sandra's apartment. John lost sight of him but kept walking and then took the same right. But walking toward Sandra's building he saw no one. *Shit*, he thought. Turning around to walk back, a man jumped out in front of him. John froze. The guy yelled, "Man, get off my back. Are you crazy? I see you at the house, and now I see you here. Do what you gotta do, but get off my back." Then the guy turned into an alley and disappeared.

Stunned, John rushed the few blocks back to his car. He opened the door, but as soon as he sat down, he felt bile rising and opened it again, vomiting. Collapsing in his seat, he remained there for about ten minutes, trying to get a grip. Finally, he drove home, feeling stupid and unnerved.

Then he remembered where he'd seen that guy from the drug house before: he'd been at Sandra's apartment building in the parking lot, talking with Jack Wilson, and later at the bar. Striker. It had to be him.

Chapter 23

BAD STUFF

Cameron, Lara, and Chad Burt met outside the courtroom at 8:30 a.m. Cameron started by saying that Amy Jo should be reunited with her family. She didn't believe that the Halstrom family was abusive; maybe the boys were rough, but not the adults. She wasn't resistant to arguments on the other side; she still didn't have enough information, the mother was unintelligible, and it was possible that Charles Halstrom was a great actor. On the other hand, his sister, Jane, was open and cooperative, and the three healthy boys showed no evidence of abuse.

"That's how I see it," Cameron concluded. "What do you think?"

Lara was in agreement, but she also looked a bit nervous, having had no involvement in this kind of decision before. Chad Burt was pragmatic, from a lawyer's standpoint, asking, "What would the judge think?"

."I've thought a great deal about that," Cameron said. "And I'm just not sure what she'll think. She seems to go against whatever I recommend lately. I like her, don't get me wrong, and I know she's tough, smart, dedicated—all the right stuff. But I don't know how to read her."

Burt said, "That's not atypical. Most of the time judges can't be read. My job is to advocate for my client. I like to think I can anticipate a judge, but they can throw curveballs. If a judge is any good, the job forces her to go to the edge of the thinking. Normally, judges return to the center."

"I never thought about it that way," Cameron said. "I'm missing something. Are you saying to forget about the judge and argue how I see it?"

"How has that worked for you so far?" Burt asked.

"Really, not too bad. Until this last week, I thought I was doing okay."

"I'm surprised to hear that," said Burt. Cameron kind of twisted her head at Burt as if wondering what that meant. She dropped it, though, saying, "Well, okay. I'll think about that."

Burt turned to Lara. "Lara, I understand you'd be nervous. But what are you thinking?"

Lara paused. All three were still standing. Lara looked over at the courtroom and then turned back to Burt and said, "I wish I knew for sure, but I don't know what the judge thinks. I'm a real estate lawyer."

Burt responded, obviously taken aback. "Sorry, bad question, sorry. I mean what do you think about the family unit, the Halstroms?"

"Okay, I can definitely answer that. Actually, I like them. The mother doesn't seem well, either physically or mentally, or maybe she's an amazing actress. But they seem like good people in general. Does that make sense?"

"Makes sense to me."

Cameron jumped in, "It makes sense to me, too, which leaves the mother. I don't think we're in a position to trust her, because we just don't know enough."

"Let's roll with that," Burt said. "We'd better go into the courtroom now."

Charles and Jane Halstrom had taken a seat in the back and were waiting for the case to be called. Fifteen minutes later, Judge Crowe walked in, and the clerk called their case.

A deputy attorney general appeared, reporting that he was stepping into the case for the first time. Judge Crowe asked if there were any others in the courtroom interested in the matter of Amy Jo Halstrom. Charles and Jane Halstrom stood and introduced themselves. They had no attorney. Judge Crowe invited them to sit at the conference table.

The courtroom remained as it always was: stark and uninviting.

Judge Crowe began. "Good morning. We're here on another shelter hearing. This means we'll consider the question as to whether the state will continue temporary custody of Amy Jo. We can countenance temporary shelter for a few days, but beyond that the state must prepare and obtain this court's approval of a plan and more permanent shelter. Mr. Halstrom, are you the father of Amy Jo?"

"Yes, ma'am," he responded.

"Ms. Jane Halstrom, I recall your appearance earlier this week. Nice to see you again. Thank you for your participation. My notes indicate the state intended to do some more investigation and that the mother, Mary Halstrom, was sick or incapacitated in some way. Ms. Springer, is there more information at this point in time?"

"Yes, your honor, we did do a follow-up. Ms. Liu and I drove to the residence and spoke with Jane and Charles Halstrom."

"Did you visit with physicians at the hospital who examined Amy Jo?"

"No, your honor, we did not."

"Why not?"

"Respectfully, Judge, given the short turnaround on this hearing, I decided to spend more time with the family in the home. There are other children—three boys—living at the home."

"Does the attorney general's office have any additional information at this time?" Judge Crowe asked.

"No, your honor, we do not. I have not spoken to Ms. Springer. We are under time constraints as well."

"Is it the intent of the attorney general's office to make inquiry and add assistance to this case?"

The deputy attorney general said the office did intend to do so.

"Well, at this time, Ms. Springer, will you please update the court and counsel on your investigation?"

"Yes, Judge." Cameron recalled the events of the day before in detail and concluded with a recommendation. "We don't have any clear understanding of the condition of Mrs. Mary Halstrom. We need more work in that respect. We don't know how Amy Jo's shoulder was broken or how the bruises occurred. Even so, it is my recommendation we work toward reunification on a step-by-step basis. I believe Ms. Liu joins in this recommendation."

Chad Burt quickly interjected, "Ms. Liu joins in that recommendation, your honor."

Cameron continued. "I base my update this morning, Judge, on the interviews Ms. Liu and I had with Jane Halstrom and Charles Halstrom. These interviews were done separately. Jane and Charles are both supportive of the family unit and are cooperative. We saw nothing of the other three children to indicate abuse. They certainly know how to play together, in a rough and tumbling way. Neither Jane nor Charles Halstrom is aware of any physical abuse, including any by the mother, Mary Halstrom. Mr. Halstrom did tell me that his wife has been in declining health, with unknown cause, for a number of weeks. Lastly, I suggest we conduct daily house visits over the weekend to ensure our recommendation of stability holds true, followed by reunification next Monday or Tuesday."

Judge Crowe turned to Mr. Burt and asked him whether he had anything to add.

"Judge," Mr. Burt said, "the guardian ad litem, Ms. Liu, agrees with the recommendation of Ms. Springer. I would like to add that with the father and aunt here before the court, if need be, we could ask some questions under oath."

"Yes, let's do that. Mr. Burt, why don't you go ahead and ask questions, followed by the deputy attorney general? Let's swear in Mr. Halstrom first, then Ms. Jane Halstrom."

The clerk swore in Mr. Halstrom, and Mr. Burt proceeded.

"Mr. Halstrom, please let me know if you don't understand any of my questions. Is that acceptable?"

"Yes, sir." He was still seated at the conference table, at the far end, with his hands in his lap. He was clean-shaven and his hair was combed, and he wore a white shirt with a bolo tie.

"Mr. Halstrom, have you ever seen your wife or sister hit or strike any of your children?"

"No, I have not."

"I understand you work on a ranch, primarily with cattle; is that correct?"

Judge Crowe interrupted. "Mr. Burt, you are leading the witness to the answer. I understand that is sometimes workable, especially to save time, but in this instance let's play by the rules."

"Yes, Judge. I will rephrase. Mr. Halstrom, are you employed?"

"Yes, I work on the Double C Ranch near Wauchula. I do most anything on the ranch needed. I work the cows, ride a horse the old-fashioned way. I do odd jobs like mending fences, digging ditches, fixing electrical and plumbing—that sort of thing. Is that what you need to know?"

"Fine, thank you very much. Now where did you grow up and how?"

"My family was farming and ranching south of Wauchula down toward Lake Okeechobee. Truth is, I grew up in the woods. I'm not educated a lot in modern ways but can do almost anything outdoors."

"Are you a hunter?"

"Yes, sir."

"Do your boys hunt?"

"Yes, not bad shots for their ages. Mostly pigs, turkeys, deer, birds."

"Have you ever had a hunting accident?"

"No, sir, nothing involving guns. Sometimes someone will fall from a tree or step in a hole. We're pretty careful to avoid swamps. We hunt alligators when allowed but try to avoid them, too. We stay out of thick palmettos if we can, try to avoid snakes although sometimes you do see them. We kill 'em."

"Have you ever taken any of your boys to the hospital for any reason?"

"Yes, each broke bones from falls and wrestling out in the yard, like a broken hand or ankle. Nothing serious."

"Have you ever hit your boys or Amy Jo?"

"No, I have not, except the boys sometimes get spanked. They're good, so it's pretty rare. They're not perfect."

"What would cause you to spank a child?"

"Stealing, hurting someone, things like that."

"Have you ever spanked for disobeying you or because they were too loud or talking back?"

"No."

"Is your wife or sister ever short with the kids, ever lost their temper?"

"No, they're too sweet, let 'em do whatever. That's a problem."

"Do you know how Amy Jo broke her shoulder?"

"No. I asked the boys, and they said they didn't know. I'm not too sure about that, but so far they haven't budged on that answer. Amy Jo didn't explain it."

"Your honor, I have no other questions," concluded Mr. Burt.

Judge Crowe turned to the deputy attorney general, a Mr. Stalnick. "Your witness," she said.

"Mr. Halstrom, I'm Attorney Stalnick, an assistant attorney general for the state of Florida. Do you understand that?"

The judge intervened again. "Mr. Stalnick, skip the histrionics. We are here to determine the best course of action for Amy Jo. Please stick to the issue."

"Yes, your honor, just wanted to make sure he understands I am here on behalf of the state of Florida."

"I'm sure he knows that."

"Mr. Halstrom, how often do you beat your kids?"

"Objection," said Burt.

"Sustained."

Mr. Stalnick told the judge he would rephrase. "Mr. Halstrom, how often do you spank your children?"

"Like I said, it's probably been a few years."

"Have you ever spanked a child by slapping in the face?"

"I don't think so."

"What do you mean, you don't think so? Do you recall slapping a child—I mean with the palm of your hand striking a child—either softly or hard?"

"I don't think so. My oldest is nine years old, so you're asking me about almost ten years ago."

"Based on your memory, is it possible?"

"Judge, I don't recall doing that, but I don't want to say something I can't recall. I roughhouse with the boys, wrestle with them, put them to bed. Maybe I slapped them in a playful way. I don't spank like that. Hard to recall spanking any of them."

Judge Crowe said, "Just answer the questions as best you can."

Mr. Stalnick continued. "Is Amy Jo old enough to walk?"

"Yes, she's three."

"Can she crawl up on furniture?"

"Yes."

"Can she pull herself over into a tub, for example?"

"Yes."

"That being the case, was there anything in the house that she could have fallen from?"

"You mean like a chair or a bed?"

"Sure."

"Yes, so long as she was on top of the bed or sitting on the chair."

"Would a fall from a chair or a bed be bad enough to break a shoulder? What do you think?"

"I don't know. One of my boys broke his arm falling off a horse. Anyway, Amy Jo is a girl."

Stalnick was working his hands on top of the table, every so often spinning a pencil in his hands or making a note and then laying down his pencil and looking up at Halstrom with his questions. He was sitting forward in his chair, a little hunched over the table. He stared at Halstrom with each question and answer.

Mr. Halstrom continued to sit straight, with hands in his lap. He held a steady gaze and didn't move or shake. He didn't look around the courtroom. He was fixed on Stalnick.

"Maybe one of your boys hit Amy Jo and knocked her over, or maybe your wife did?"

"What? You're crazy. That didn't happen."

"How do you know that?"

"'Cause I know they would never do that."

"Did you ask your boys what happened?"

"Yes, I did."

"How did you do that?"

"I said they better tell me the truth or else they would get it."

"Get what?"

"A whipping."

"Is a whipping the same as a spanking?"

"Yes. A whipping is with a switch."

"What kind of a switch?"

"Anything: a stick, a towel; I don't know."

"I have no further questions."

Judge Crowe said she had heard enough testimony. She asked Mr. Burt to provide his clients' thoughts.

"Judge, Ms. Liu and Caseworker Springer are in agreement that in the next few days Amy Jo should return to her family. There is no evidence of any prior abuse reported to DCF or anyone, no evidence the father, mother, or aunt hit the child. The family has been together for over ten years without any sort of criminal arrests, and there is no evidence of drug abuse. Mr. Halstrom has had a steady job for many years. This isn't the time to be second-guessing and wondering what might have happened. Mr. Stalnick's questions are designed to suggest that maybe something happened and maybe someone is lying. But it is strictly conjecture and speculation."

Mr. Stalnick replied, "Judge, a lot of things can happen, and we've seen cases in this courtroom where kids end up hurt, injured, even murdered. Cases like this need certainty. I know Ms. Springer and Ms. Liu mean well. In reality, Ms. Springer works for the state through a private service organization, Kids Care Inc., and in that sense my position on behalf of the state is contradicted by Ms. Springer as a representative of the state. From the standpoint of the state of Florida, as represented by me, the state does not think the child should return to the home anytime soon."

"All right," Judge Crowe said. "My ruling is that Ms. Springer and Ms. Liu need to do more research. I like the idea of family monitoring over the weekend and thereafter for a few days. Maybe they can get to the bottom of this. In the meantime, Amy Jo remains in state custody, in temporary care. Now, Mr. Halstrom and Ms. Halstrom, this ruling is temporary. Be patient and let these professionals do their job. No one at this time is threatening to take your child for good. Can you continue to cooperate?"

Jane Halstrom spoke up. "Judge, I think this is terrible and that the lawyer for the state is terrible. He's never been to the house, knows nothing, and now he's just asking a bunch of mean questions. I don't want to promise anything. I'm sure you're a good lady and a good judge, but this is very bad, very bad stuff."

Judge Crowe asked, "Mr. Halstrom, do you have anything to say?" He stood up from the conference table, hands by his side, silently, and then looked up and haltingly said, "No, ma'am." He sat back down. Jane, sitting beside him, put her arm around his shoulders and reached out for his hand. She whispered something in his ear, and then they both stood and walked out.

Everyone looked at them. The room was quiet. Stalnick shuffled his papers and quickly followed them out. Judge Crowe watched too. After they left, she looked over to Cameron with a solemn expression and gave a slight nod. Cameron felt charged up: she would carry forward for an accurate, just resolution. Her fight had just begun. She left the courtroom and headed to her office.

Chapter 24

CONNECTIONS

John was in his cubicle, waiting for Cameron after the hearing. "How'd it go?" he asked, peering around the corner as Cameron threw her purse down.

Cameron didn't want to talk; she'd talked enough in court, and it had amounted to nothing. Stalnick had undercut her position. At least Judge Crowe had accepted her recommendation for more fieldwork. She was still mystified by the cowboy. He seemed like a nice guy, but he had no answers and no hesitation about spanking and switching. There would be more fieldwork.

"We have more work to do over the weekend, or at least I do," she called out over the cubicle. "Judge Crowe accepted my recommendation for that. Still no clarity. That state's deputy attorney Stalnick showed up and grilled Halstrom. All this stuff about spanking and switching came out, so reunification early next week seems a lost cause for now." She put her elbows on the table and sank her head into her palms.

"So what can be done about Stalnick?" John asked.

Cameron got up and walked around to John and leaned against his cubicle. "We need to turn him to our side," Cameron replied. "I may be forced to work with him on this—every case is hard right now."

"You got that right. Well, we have the ball game on Sunday. Something fun. Let's get an early lunch." John spun his chair around to face Cameron. "We're out of here." He grabbed Cameron's hand and pulled her out into the hallway.

"Okay," she said. "Don't pull my arm out of the socket, Rocket Man." They found a Cuban restaurant in West Tampa near downtown and placed their order. It was the kind of food in Tampa that was always on the stove and ready to eat. Everyone around them was speaking fast, indecipherable Spanish.

Energized by the food and the fun of John dragging her out to the café, Cameron sat back in her chair—her hands on top of the table, her head cocked to the side with a big smile, eyes wide open with excitement—and did a 180 with the conversation. "Listen, about Tuesday night at Sam's. You were sullen; you know what I mean?"

John sighed. "I'm sorry about that. You know sometimes it's like I shrink into a hole."

"I mean, I can too," Cameron admitted. "It's just that lately it seems like you've said nothing about your free time, except for mentioning Sam's or baseball. But you know you can call me, right? It's better than just always work, don't you think?"

"Uh, okay, if you say so," John said and then sat there, obviously not knowing what else to say. He twisted in his chair and sat up a little.

"It's not like we can't do some fun stuff," Cameron said. "Look, I just can't let you turn into a hermit, okay?"

"I will not turn into a hermit; I promise," John said, smiling now. "And you're right to call me out on it. You really are a good friend to me; I love that about you. Thanks."

"You're welcome."

They sat in companionable silence for a minute and then John said, "Well, you know, now that we've got all personal, I do have to say I've definitely stepped out of my element. Somehow I've turned into Joe Friday the cop." Cameron frowned a little at that.

John said, sheepishly and with a touch of guilt, "I haven't told you about last night." He looked at Cameron. "I guess I'd better."

"What?"

"I went to the hospital last night to see Sandra. She was asleep. So, nothing there. I was wired, so I drove over to Suitcase City and staked out that bar I've been to."

"All right, give me the details," Cameron said. "I'm a little concerned."

"That guy who keeps popping up everywhere—at Sandra's, at the drug house—he showed up last night," John went on. "He obviously has some sort of connection to Sandra, because I figured out where I'd seen him before. It was when we were speaking with Sandra's neighbors, the Reeds. He was with Jack Wilson down in the courtyard."

With that, Cameron perked up. "Okay, so what does that mean?"

"So while I'm in the car, he turns up again, heading in the direction of Sandra's place. I followed him for about three blocks. It was around 10:00."

"And then what?"

John shrugged, wondering if he should give her all the details. She seemed really angry, and he didn't know why. "Well, I lost him," he admitted. "But then he jumped out of the dark and screamed at me, saying I was crazy and needed to get off his back."

"Are you serious? John, that isn't good. Not at all."

Cameron abruptly got up from the table and left. John stayed there for a while, trying to sort things out. What was Cameron's problem? They'd been talking about this stuff all along, and they both knew that investigating anything carried risk. Maybe he shouldn't be tailing people at night and nosing around, but still. Her attitude was perplexing. He sat there for another hour, sipping café con leche, and then he finally got up and caught a taxi to the hospital.

———

Sandra was awake. She was still bruised and sorry looking, but she was sitting up in bed. John asked permission to come in, and she said yes.

"The police told me you saved me," she said to him, looking grateful.

He hadn't thought about it that way. "Thanks, but truthfully, I didn't. I just happened to be there. Your neighbors, the Reeds, called, and I called the cops. Do you mind if I ask you who did this, uh, or is it too soon to get into?"

"You can ask, but I don't know," she replied. "I really don't know. I don't remember anything."

"Okay," John said. "Keep it up, that's great."

"How's David? I can't wait to see him. I'm worried."

"He's fine. He's got good care. I get a report every day through the computer system. You really don't remember?"

Sandra shook her head. "No. I tried to remember when the cops came earlier today. I remember watching some TV. I must have fallen asleep. Next thing I know, I woke up here."

"I'm glad I got there," John said. "Do you feel like talking anymore?"

She laid her head back on the bed and closed her eyes. "Have you seen David?" she asked.

"No, just the reports. Do you want me to visit him? I'm happy to do that."

"Please, can I see him? Can he come to the hospital?"

"I don't know. I'll have to check." He touched the side of the bed, leaned over, and said, "You get well. David's fine."

She said that she needed to sleep, so he asked one last question. "Do you know a guy named Striker?"

"I don't know. I don't feel good." She closed her eyes.

He decided to come back later that day, maybe tomorrow. And he'd go check up on David. Maybe it would lead to something.

He felt a little better. He'd done a good thing. He forgot about Cameron for a moment, because the feeling of trying to help felt good.

Chapter 25

NINETY-NINE-CENT HAMBURGERS

After leaving John at the lunch place, Cameron went back to her office and shuffled through paperwork and computer entries on FinCen. She entered an up-to-date case note for Alisha Santeroa, indicating that John had continued to search for information on Juan Martinez but had gathered nothing directly relevant. Elijah was reunited with Alisha and his grandmother, and Cameron would conduct another home visit soon. That done, she headed off for Alisha's apartment. John was still not back at the office, which was too bad: she felt she needed to apologize for her snappiness at lunch.

When she knocked at Alisha's door, it was Juan Martinez who opened it. "Oh, you again. Alisha's not here. She's out job hunting. Elijah's asleep."

"All good; sorry to miss her," Cameron said. "I hope she's well. And Elijah?"

"Good, took him to the park, hung out. It was good. Off work at noon, caught a bus back."

"Okay. Thanks for the report. You know I have concerns about you—that's obvious. That's not a surprise. Nothing personal, but my job is to be on guard, and you were angry." She was standing outside, aware she was alone with Martinez, who she had thought was violent and dangerous.

"I'm still angry," he said, "but glad Elijah's back home. Alisha's a good mom; she loves that kid. I still don't get how you can just walk into somebody's home and take their child. I don't like it, and I'm not happy you did it." He didn't invite her into the apartment, even though his demeanor was basically friendly.

"Look," he said, "maybe you should get to know me. I'm not a bad guy. We're both here; why don't we talk for a few minutes? Okay?"

"Sure." Maybe her instincts were telling her that Juan wasn't a problem after all. "You know Elijah has been a child subject to our monitoring from the day he was born, right?"

He said he did know, and also knew about Alisha's first child, born when Alisha was fourteen. He knew she had once been into drugs, but now she had a good thing going with her mother.

"Okay," Cameron said. So far, he wasn't saying anything out of line. "I need to learn more about you, Mr. Martinez. This is important."

"I work at the docks," he said. "Work can be on and off. I'm from New York City, been here three years. Haven't had any problems. I have an apartment and cell phone, no car. I walk, bum rides, take the bus, if and when I can. I've never served any time."

"Been arrested?" Cameron asked, cocking her head down and looking up at him with her eyebrows raised.

"Yes."

"For what?"

"Battery. I was homeless in New York and hit a rough spot. So they put me on supervision for a while. It was a bar fight. I stayed out of trouble after that, so probation."

"How did you meet Alisha?"

"I was eating ninety-nine-cent hamburgers when I got down here, and she was always waiting on me. That was about six months ago. We became friends and went out some, nothing serious. Why don't you come in and sit for a few minutes?" She walked in and sat down. Juan sat across the room from her.

"Ever take an anger management course?" she asked.

"What the hell is that—are you bullshitting me?"

"No, it's for real. Maybe I can get you into one of the courses we work with?"

Juan shrugged. "I don't care, but if they serve coffee and some food, I'd go for it. I'll need to walk there. I dunno. I'm not an angry guy."

"Well, we'd find out at least. I know you must like Alisha, because it seems you take care of Elijah and you're around, but what do you know about her?"

"Just what I told you. She's young. We're having a good time. She's nice. A straight talker, sensitive. She overcame drugs: that's a big deal. We're just good friends. I look after her and her kid."

"Okay, I get that. Thanks. Have you ever been in a fight with her mother, or do you have fights with Alisha?"

"The mother's not around much. She's always picking up the kid during the day. I hardly see her. She doesn't say much to me—picks up Elijah and leaves. Anyway, mostly I'm at the docks or here. I leave at 4:30 in the morning. Sometimes I sleep over here on the couch. My place is around the corner."

"Is it the two of you now, Mr. Martinez?"

"As far as I know, the answer is no. Maybe we're working on it, but I don't really know."

At that point, Alisha showed up. "Well, look at the two of you. Sitting down for a cup of tea, are you?"

"Not quite," Cameron said. "I'm getting ready to leave. I was just paying a home visit. How are you? How's the job search coming? You look good, very professional." She smiled approvingly at Alisha, who was wearing a pair of black slacks and a loose-fitting blue blouse with an open collar.

"Thanks," Alisha said. "It was a good day today. I had an interview with a nonprofit that takes care of abused women. Got the reference from my program teacher."

"Wow, great. I like to hear that," Cameron said, standing up. "Best of luck with that, and I'll see you later."

Alisha smiled and said thanks.

"I appreciate the time, Mr. Martinez," Cameron said, going to the door.

She headed back to the office to see if John had shown up.

Chapter 26

ANOTHER CAFÉ CON LECHE

John was back in the field. He looked up his police friends and joined them for a cup of coffee at the Tropicana Café in Ybor City, the historic Hispanic and Latin quarter of Tampa. It was the best place to see people, be seen, and enjoy a Cuban sandwich or a cup of black beans or, to spice things up, a deviled crab with hot sauce. His two cop friends were there on a break. Yes, they had looked for Jack Wilson, they told him. The department had distributed his profile and issued an APB for Wilson but had come up with nothing. And they'd questioned his so-called sister, who denied any knowledge of his whereabouts.

The guy known as Striker was a different story. They had no information on his real name or his address. They had interviewed some people at the house on Twenty-Second Street. No one knew him or admitted they knew him, which the police didn't believe. No one gave an inch of cooperation. In their experience working the neighborhood, they had never heard of a Striker or run across anyone of his description.

John told them about his brief encounter at Sandra's apartment complex and his altercation with Striker the night before, when he'd jumped out of the darkness and given John fair warning. "I mean, it wasn't really an altercation," he explained.

"Unfortunately, there's not enough for an APB with him," one of the cops said.

It was starting to look like a dead end to John. If the cops couldn't find Wilson or Striker, why would he have better luck? For his purposes, the question was whether Sandra was still in danger. No one knew for sure who the perp was. And the danger could easily include her son, David, so it was best to leave him in temporary shelter and Sandra in the hospital for now. But what about Alisha, Elijah, and the boyfriend, Juan Martinez? He had nothing on him either. Wondering what to do now—and as a last-ditch effort and maybe his last chance to play Joe Friday—he decided to drive to the café where he'd heard about the drug house.

He walked into the café at about 4:00 p.m., took a seat at the bar, and ordered another café con leche. His cover was to peruse the day's paper, which amounted to nothing. As usual, he read and digested the sports section, including information on the Sunday Rays game. He was looking forward to that.

He hardly lasted an hour at the café, his head buried in the paper but neither thinking nor reading. He began to fidget and finally decided he couldn't resist calling Cameron.

"Where are you?" she asked. She didn't sound irritated anymore, which relieved him.

"Nowhere interesting. I'm headed back to the office."

"You won't believe this, but I had a good conversation with Juan Martinez."

"Really? That's great. At least you uncovered something on Martinez, I assume, straight from the horse's mouth."

"Not a ton," Cameron said, "but he did open up some to me. He sounded credible, I have to say. I think he'll give us more. We just need to set up something more official."

"Fine, it's a workable plan. And sorry if I worried you earlier, by the way. I didn't mean to."

"No, I'm sorry," Cameron said.

"Thanks. Look—I'm thinking I should join you on the next home visit to the Halstroms. You know, get back out there with you and the alligators."

"Okay, first thing in the morning. Lara will join us."

"Sounds good."

There didn't seem to be anything more to say, so John decided to go straight home and skip the office. He was still worn out from discovering Sandra naked and curled up in a ball, and his scare with Striker had added salt to the wound. He never should have told Cameron about the incident and didn't blame her for being upset. Striker. It was so curious, the way the guy kept popping up. When would be next?

Chapter 27

NOT AN ANIMAL

On Friday night, Striker drifted, wondering where he would sleep. He knew he shouldn't intrude again on Alisha. The Spaniard was probably hanging around. It was hard to say what that guy was—friend, lover, babysitter? Anyway, he wouldn't go back there anytime soon. And Sandra was nowhere. Just disappeared. Around 9:00 p.m., he ran into Jack Wilson, who jumped out from behind a hedgerow.

"Shit!" Striker exclaimed. "Man, don't do that again. You scared me. Some White guy followed me the other night. I think we saw him Tuesday night at Sandra's place. He was there with a woman. Very pretty."

"Yeah," Wilson said, "I know who you're talking about. I ran into him at a bar, told him to get out—he was going to get himself killed. I met him before at Sandra's. He was with the woman then, too. I'd like to meet her again—underneath me."

"Forget that. It's trouble."

"Look, man, they're child welfare workers. They took Sandra's kid, or someone did. The woman was all over Sandra the other night. She's got all this do-gooder shit going on." Wilson was looking all around. He was dirty and smelly, just as Striker usually was. Striker was his typical unkempt self but calm and relaxed walking around the neighborhood.

"Jack, why're you hiding behind bushes?"

"Listen, man, what up? You're the one staying away and barking against the Man. I'm just following your lead. I feel like I need to stay low. I'm outta here sooner or later."

"What for? Where's Sandra?"

"Man, forget her. That bitch is over."

"What? She's nice, a good kid. I like her. Where is she? I thought you were her man, you know, the two of you. I didn't like it—just a fact. Looks like I was right."

Wilson shook his head and leaned down from his waist, looking at the ground. "Not now, don't want to talk about her." He winced, bending down to rub his ankle. Striker took note. Wilson said, "Took a bad fall. Anyway, glad to be out of her hair. Had to get away from bad stuff, like to kill me. I took full advantage of the night, like you."

"That does sound like me," Striker admitted.

"Look, I'm not an animal, but, yeah, I crawled around and found an abandoned house, got some food. Saw some cops, nothing unusual."

"What the fuck you done? Forget it, man; I don't want to know."

"Nothing, I done nothing. You know I don't deal—too risky." Then, for some reason, he started telling Striker about his "fucked-up family"—the usual stuff: absent father, neglectful mother.

Striker shook his head. "Man, why are you telling me all this? I'm not a shrink. But, I mean, I'll listen if it helps."

"Striker, thanks, yeah, you're a good friend. I like talkin'. You got that?" Wilson reached out to Striker with both hands, still bent over, like he wanted a hug or a handshake.

Striker wasn't going to touch him; he knew that for sure. He thought

Wilson was acting out; maybe he was doped up. Striker wasn't sure. "You liked Sandra," Striker said.

"But I'm not going to put up with her anymore. Who's she kidding, paying attention to that bitch social worker and her little boyfriend, coworker, whatever he is."

Striker walked off, leaving Wilson alone, not liking the talk about Sandra. He wasn't upset that they'd broken up. *It's a good thing*, he thought.

It was one in the morning when he finally left.

Chapter 28

STICKS

On Saturday morning, John, Cameron, and Lara headed over to the Halstroms', arriving about 11:00 a.m. John was in jeans and a short-sleeved shirt with no collar. His black hair was getting a bit long and hung over his ears. Lara, the consummate professional, wore a dark-blue skirt and white blouse. Cameron had on a pair of nice jeans and a loose-fitting pink-and-blue blouse.

"I'm wearing jeans next time," Lara said, laughing. "Don't worry. I'll learn."

All three Halstrom boys were in the yard roughhousing, jumping on each other and boxing. "Is that a bit rough?" Lara asked as they pulled up. "I don't know."

The bigger boy wrestled the smaller one to the ground and applied a restraint hold for a second before releasing. The smaller one took off, running headlong into the third boy, who had been happily yelling words of encouragement to the two fighters.

Cameron said, "Well, let's get inside." A short distance beyond, an alligator was sunning on the bank of the slough, but Cameron was growing accustomed to wild things, and this time it didn't bother her.

Jane opened the front door and invited them in.

Glancing back at the boys—all three then wound in a big ball—Cameron remarked, "Those boys are certainly having a good time!"

Jane said, "This stuff goes on all day, except I hope not when they're in school. Good morning. We're all here."

The three followed Jane into the kitchen, where Mary and Charles Halstrom were waiting.

"Good morning," Cameron said. "Thanks for meeting with us again. We're sorry for the intrusion. You may remember the judge told us to visit you this weekend, each day, so here we are. You remember my coworker, John Quint, and you know Ms. Liu."

John said, "Nice to see you again. Hope you don't mind me joining Lara and Cameron today."

"No problem," Charles Halstrom said. "Let's get on with your business."

"Mr. Halstrom, we don't have anything in particular to cover this morning," Cameron said. "We're just checking in to make sure everything's okay. Is there anything you want to tell us? How was last night? How were the boys? We see they're back at it this morning, raising Cain."

"I told you they do roughhouse," Charles Halstrom said. "At least they appreciate each other and the outdoors."

Cameron turned her eyes to Mary Halstrom. "I hope your day is going well," she said. Mrs. Halstrom raised her eyes and then lowered them. *Well*, Cameron thought, *at least some reaction.* "Nice to see you again. You must be proud of your boys." Mrs. Halstrom gave a brief nod and continued to look down.

Jane Halstrom spoke up. "Why don't we walk into the backyard."

"Good, I like the fresh air," John said.

"Great, but do you mind if we look around the house, too?" Cameron asked. "This is typical procedure, and we need to tell the judge we did so. She'd expect that."

"Fine." Jane proceeded to escort them through the house. There were only two bedrooms. Things were a bit sloppy, but there was nothing untoward. They walked outside. Mary Halstrom didn't move from the table.

Once out in the backyard, Cameron steeled herself to ask a difficult question. "Would you mind if we ask a social worker, maybe a psychologist, to interview your wife? It would be helpful to us, and maybe to you as well."

Surprisingly, Halstrom didn't push back. "Do what you have to do. A professional might be helpful."

"All right, thanks. I promise you it won't be intrusive."

"Maybe you can get something out of her. She doesn't talk no more."

"How about I do a quick interview of her right now, just the two of us? Would you mind that?"

"No, go ahead."

Jane said, "I guess that's fine, but I'm worried about her. Is that really a good idea? Maybe I should go inside and at least ask her."

"Okay," Cameron said.

Jane went in while the others remained outside, waiting. After a few minutes, Jane reported that she seemed fine, so Cameron could go ahead. Inside, Cameron sat at the dinette table, her remarks slow but deliberate, her voice calm.

"Mrs. Halstrom, thanks. I'll be brief. Is that okay?" Mary Halstrom said nothing and continued to look down. "Is there anything you want to tell me?" Mary didn't move or respond. Cameron waited for a few minutes but, realizing she wasn't going to get a further response, decided to cut the interview short. "Take care. I'll leave you alone now. Thank you."

Cameron returned to the others outside. "She's not responsive. I'll get the professional to help. One last thing: Do we have your permission to talk to the boys as a group in your presence? I think that would be helpful to you and Amy Jo."

Charles Halstrom shuffled his feet and walked off. "Let me think about that." He walked around the house, and in about three minutes returned with the boys. "Here they are," he said.

Cameron continued, since it seemed like John and Lara were content to stay quiet as backups. "Thanks, guys. My name is Cameron, and these are my friends, Lara and John. We would like you to help us. We are working with Amy Jo and need your help. Is that okay?"

The older boy said, "Sure."

"Do you think Amy Jo is a good sister?"

"Yes," said the older boy, and the other two nodded vigorously. The older boy stood in a position of attention, hands by his side. The two younger ones stood likewise, rocking slightly back and forth in place.

"Do you guys like her? Is she fun to hang out with, even though she's younger?"

"Sure," they both said. The youngest added, "She's fun." They both wore worn-out blue jeans with white T-shirts, evidently clean except for dirt from the morning's play. They were barefoot. They were slim and strong, with sandy-brown hair and big, wide smiles.

"You know she has a broken shoulder?"

"Yes, ma'am," they responded in unison. The younger one pitched in again, saying, "Dad and Aunt Jane told us that. She came back from the hospital. Did you take her away?"

"Well, we did that just to make sure her shoulder heals. She's fine and doing well. We hope to bring her back soon."

They didn't respond except to look slightly confused, shuffle their feet in place, and look around at their father and aunt.

"Thanks, guys. You're very polite. Thanks a bunch. Have fun this weekend."

Charles Halstrom said, "Scram, but don't leave the yard. Lunch will be soon. Don't go near the swamp."

They hightailed it to the bigger yard out front.

"Mr. Halstrom, Jane, thank you," said Cameron. "We'll be going now. Appreciate your time. We'll be back in touch soon about the social worker visit and see you again tomorrow. How about in the morning?" She smiled. "Baseball game in the afternoon."

"Make it early," Mr. Halstrom said. "We have church at 10:00."

"Yes, sir. Thanks," said Cameron. As they drove away, they noticed that the boys were back to boxing, this time throwing sticks at each other as well.

Lara drove again. John said, "Well, I get what you've been talking about. Interesting. And there they are again: the alligators. Wow."

"Yeah, I see the alligators," Cameron responded. "Believe it or not, I'm getting used to them."

"So we still don't really have anything," Lara said as they neared the interstate. "I mean, I think they're pretty open. They're a family. They go to church on Sunday mornings."

"I wonder what kind of church," John said.

"I still don't get the mother," Cameron said. "Maybe she's faking her whole act and is really in charge, like a cult bishop or something? I'm kidding, but you know? What's up with her?"

Lara said, "Maybe I'm wrong, but my instinct says the father is good-hearted. Maybe he doesn't know how to deal with a mentally ill wife. The boys seem normal to me—obviously wild-spirited, but I mean, they're just boys."

"Look, it'll all come down to what this shrink or social worker says," John told them. "At this point, we have no real evidence of child abuse. We have one three-year-old with a broken shoulder no one can explain, and we have an opinion of potential abuse by some medical professional at the hospital, but do they have a basis for that? The girl could have fallen off the front porch or found herself in the middle of a wrestling match."

Cameron said, "Basically, it sounds like we're on the same wavelength. We just need to get a shrink involved as soon as possible. Let's go to Sam's tonight and have a drink; I could use one. Lara, you're invited."

Lara looked at both of them, clearly pleased to be included. "Sure!" she said. "But can one of you pick me up? I don't want to show up on my own."

John said, "Sure." Knowing they still had more to learn, the three continued back to the city, looking forward to a good time that night.

Chapter 29

COMPETITION

By the time Lara and John arrived at Sam's it was around 10:00 p.m. Daniel and Nick were already sitting at the bar, downing beers. John spotted them and immediately wondered where Cameron was. He was forced to introduce Lara on his own.

"Nick, Daniel, good to see you. This is Lara. She's been helping us on a case. Where's Cameron?"

"Not sure," said Nick. "Late, I guess. Glad to see you guys." Reaching out his hand, he said to Lara, "Nice to meet you."

Daniel did likewise. "Lara, this is great. I like the dynamics. Three ugly guys and one beautiful woman."

"Of course Daniel is going to ply you with compliments—well deserved, I might add," Nick said. "Make sure you give him attention, or you'll never get rid of him."

"I see you guys are best friends," Lara replied.

"Well, not so fast. We're competitors."

"Competition? At what? Or are you guys playing the male thing at the saloon, and I'm the only female? So I get it now. That said, so far, John's the only one in the race!" Lara grinned. "Sorry, I can't believe I said that."

John was pleasantly surprised. *I'll take it,* he thought.

Lara grabbed John's arm and leaned into him, saying, "Do I need protection?"

John didn't know what to do, but he gave it his best shot. "From these guys, not really." Everyone laughed. Daniel and Nick in unison raised their glasses and offered, "Touché!"

Nick grabbed John by the shoulder. "Hey, what's the line on the Rays tomorrow? I think they have a good chance. They've got that young guy, Longoria. He's off to a great start."

John said, "Good point. That guy's going to be great—good attitude, plays third base, maybe another Mike Schmidt from the Phillies."

"Schmidt: ages ago, I mean, a long time ago, Hall of Famer," Daniel put in. "Really, that strong? You're stepping out with that prediction. You sure you can out-baseball Nick and me?"

"Yeah, wait and see."

"Hope so," Daniel said. "Schmidt was the greatest third baseman of all time."

"That's right," John said.

Nick sidled over to Lara. "So, you work with Cameron and John?"

"On this case, yes, but mostly I'm a real estate lawyer downtown. And I can't talk baseball."

Daniel suggested they move to a table for four. Lara sat between John and Nick. They got the last four-top. The bar was full, and country music was playing: mostly Dolly Parton, Garth Brooks, and old-timers like Merle Haggard and George Jones.

After the talk drifted to baseball and Lara started to tune out, Daniel turned his attention to her. "Interesting combo," he said to her. "Child welfare and real estate law, I mean. What's that about?" He pulled his seat a little closer.

Lara shrugged. "It just happened," she said. "I wanted to do some pro bono and working for kids sounded good." She looked around, sitting up in her chair. Daniel and Nick nodded approval, and Daniel said, "That sounds right."

"I wonder where Cameron is," Lara said, looking around. "Am I going to be stuck with you three all night?" She smiled.

"Who knows?" Daniel said. "But you may as well make the best of it. How about another round?"

"Sounds good." Lara held up her empty glass. "I'm game."

"Coming right up," Daniel said. "One for you too, John?"

"Great. Thanks."

Lara turned to Nick. "So what keeps you busy?"

"Sad to say," Nick said. "I'm into real estate—I work for a developer. I moved here a year ago after graduating from the University of Kentucky. I'm originally from Lexington, but I always wanted to live in Florida. Anyway, I assume you know all about real estate deals."

"Yes, way too much. How about you?" She turned to Daniel, who handed her a beer.

"Me, I try not to work," Daniel said. "My favorite place is Sam's. I work, of course. Not really a bad job; I like it, selling and buying mortgages for financial institutions like banks, savings and loans, that sort of stuff. It's a crazy market with the financial meltdown last year—actually still melted, for all intents and purposes."

"I know about that, too," Lara said. "I do some work on construction loans for apartments, condos, that kind of stuff. Sometimes I get into the details of construction documents and see what the project managers actually do."

"We get sued, that's for sure!" Daniel said. "And I have to meet with the lawyers. You're everywhere."

Lara laughed. "True, even in the wilds of Florida. That's where I went this morning with John and Cameron, to meet a family about their children."

"Tell me about it," Daniel said.

"It's confidential. I wish I could. I can't get the case out of my mind. I suppose that's good: something to think about other than how a real estate contract is written or whether a closing statement has the correct numbers. I guarantee your job is more interesting."

"Who do you work with?" Daniel asked.

"I like the firm I'm with—pretty traditional and not diverse enough, but overall it's a nice place to work. I think I'm the only minority lawyer there."

"Listen," Daniel said, "how about you join us at the Rays game tomorrow? It's fun. Plus, beer and hot dogs."

John was getting more comfortable, even though he was virtually tongue-tied. He still wanted to know where Cameron was. "Yeah, Lara, you should join us," he said. *That actually would be fun*, he thought. It would even things out a bit, make it easier to be there with Nick and Daniel.

"That'd be great!" Lara said. She looked at John. "Will we be finished up in time at the Halstroms'?"

"We should be," he assured her.

"Then I'm in! And I'll read up a little tonight. I know the Rays play in St. Pete across the bay, but that's about it."

"Tonight?" Nick said. "Are you kidding? We're going to be up until tomorrow. This is shaping up to be a long night, and there's no bailing now."

"Well, late for me," Lara said. "What do you think, John?"

"I can make it till midnight," he replied.

"Works for me," Lara said. "And can you pick me up again?"

"No problem." John was in heaven. *Maybe*, he thought, *I'm getting some mojo.* It was a nice feeling. But Cameron's absence was puzzling. Finally, at 11:00 p.m., he stepped outside to call her.

There was no answer. He waited five minutes and called again. Nothing. Now his mind began to churn even more. He was worried about her and wondered where Jack Wilson and Striker were. They knew about John, so they had to know about Cameron too. He started walking to his car, texting, "Where are you?"

Then his phone pinged. "Home, sleep @ 8:00, just crashed. See you a.m."

He went back to the bar. "Can you believe it? Cameron fell asleep at 8:00. She's all right. Lara, how about we go now? Early rise tomorrow."

"Fine. See you guys, and thanks for all the fun." Nick and Daniel looked disappointed.

"I was getting worried about her," John said.

"And you were leaving me to the wolves!" She smiled at him again, clearly being playful.

He smiled at her, too. "Lara, the chances of me abandoning you were zero."

Chapter 30

A BROTHER

On Sunday morning, John bailed as the driver, leaving Lara with the task. She picked up Cameron and John in that order, flipped on the AC, and drove the three to the Halstroms'. They were all rested and ready to go, enjoying their newfound friendship and feeling relaxed.

During the ride, John kept thinking about Striker and Jack Wilson, as well as Juan Martinez, and now there was Charles Halstrom. All of them were mysteries in some way. And the women involved with them clearly loved their children—though in the case of Mary Halstrom, it was hard to tell. The de facto surrogate mother in that situation was clearly Aunt Jane.

What to make of this, John wondered. They still knew so little about the men. None of them felt good about Striker or Wilson, but maybe they were missing something with Halstrom. And according to Cameron, there was now something leaning in favor of Martinez. Nobody was perfect. Charles Halstrom had a disturbed wife for sure. Was he the cause? None of it was easy to decipher.

"John, you're awfully quiet," Cameron said. "You comfortable back there?"

"Yeah, I'm good. You two are just chatting away up there. I'm happy."

"Well, enjoy your solitude."

A few minutes later, he said, "I'm thinking about Charles Halstrom. He seems pretty much okay. But are we missing something?"

"I don't know," Cameron said. "All we have is a few days of information. Nothing that bad really, just a hospital hotline tip and zoned-out wife."

"I wonder if we should interrogate him more. I'm spending all this time running around town to get stuff on Wilson and Striker, and you spoke directly with Martinez yesterday. I know you interviewed Charles Halstrom earlier. Is there any harm in pushing him a bit more?"

"I don't know," Cameron said. "I can't tell how much he's willing to be pushed."

Lara kept driving. "I'm listening and thinking," she said. "Would it hurt to talk more to Mr. Halstrom?"

"Well, just think about it," said Cameron. "At the hearing on Friday, the judge basically continued to rule against him. He doesn't seem like the kind of guy to roll over and play dead."

Cameron stared straight ahead, thinking. Maybe she should back off, let John take the lead. He was technically her boss, after all. "Look, I defer to you," she said. "Play it by ear, okay? Go ahead with it, but be careful. I'm okay with it. Charles Halstrom is no fool, that's for sure."

Near the Halstrom house, two alligators lay on the swamp bank, steely eyed, without a single movement. They were all getting used to the wildlife, but even so, they hurried gingerly to the front door.

Charles and his wife, Mary, were in the kitchen, and the boys were getting ready for church. Jane was not there. The kitchen was once again spotless: no dishes in the sink or on the countertops. Someone had cleaned up after breakfast.

After exchanging pleasantries, Charles said, "You showed up at a good time. I finished the dishes a few minutes ago, and the kids ran on outside. How's Amy Jo?"

"Good. We got a report this morning. She's rested and playful. What'd you have for breakfast?" Cameron asked. "I smell some bacon or sausage, and I see the orange juice."

"A full breakfast," he said. "The works. Too bad Amy Joe's not here."

"I wish I'd been here earlier," John said. "I'm sure it was better than my granola bar."

"You'd be welcome. You could bring Amy Jo with you."

"That's the goal," Cameron said. "Listen, Mr. Halstrom, as we said before, we're here to do a check-in, like we discussed before with Judge Crowe. Everything looks good. Maybe you'll let me say hello to the boys? In the meantime, I know my boss, John Quint, here would like to chat with you."

The boys were cordial and somewhat formal with Cameron. They looked cute in their Sunday best, all cleaned up for church.

John and Charles stepped outside into the backyard.

"Mr. Halstrom, as Cameron said, I'm her boss, but that's more of a technicality than reality. The fact is we, as a team, are working hard to get Amy Jo back to you as soon as possible. We're not really comfortable with the removal of her to state's shelter. So, just to firm things up, I thought I should have a deeper discussion with you."

"Can we make it quick? We're headed to church."

"I'll get on with it," John said. "Do teachers or other family members or church people—does anyone have contact with Amy Jo?"

"No, not really."

"Does she go to school or have outside care at all?"

"She stays home, just with family. She's too young for school."

John nodded.

"Mary does have a brother," Halstrom went on. "He just left the area."

"Really, I didn't know that." Who was he referring to? John wondered.

"No, he's not around anymore. I think he's gone, or he should be gone. I saw him after the hearing on Friday." Charles Halstrom stood erect, not moving, and stared straight at John.

"Had he been around the house, I mean, last week?" John asked, walking around the yard, looking for more wildlife. He didn't see any.

"He was here yesterday afternoon, Saturday, after you all left."

"Before then?" John turned around and looked at Halstrom.

"No."

The backyard, smaller than the front, looked more like the beginning of swamp and broad piney woods.

"You sure? He's gone now, just after yesterday? What's his story?"

"Not good."

"You think he was around Amy Jo last Tuesday, when Amy Jo was in the hospital? I'm just checking." John continued to walk around, looking everywhere and asking questions, only occasionally looking over at Halstrom.

"Fair's fair. Yeah, nowhere near her. I know that."

"For certain?"

"About as certain as a shot snake is dead."

"What does that mean, *a shot snake?*"

"The man is a snake, but no way he hurt Amy Jo."

"Mr. Halstrom, I'm ready to listen."

"I got nothing to hide."

"Good, let's hear it."

"Yesterday, after you left, Jane and I went to the store. We came back, and as we drove down the dirt road up to the yard, there was

Mary's brother, Richard, sitting up on the tailgate of his truck. Jane went into the house. I told Richard he should stay away. He told me to go fuck myself and that he's off to New Orleans. Said he'd never be back. Far as I'm concerned, that's a good thing. I told him he should thank me for being such a good shot."

"What does that mean?" John asked.

Halstrom shook his head. "That's another story," he said. "I asked Richard how long he'd been at the house. He said he didn't go in, that he was in the yard for about an hour and that he didn't see Mary. That's when I asked him if he'd touched Amy Jo. He said he didn't, and I told him that he better be right about that."

"Okay," John said. "Did you believe him?"

"Fact is," Charles said, "I never caught Richard in a lie. So Amy Jo must just have fallen somehow. The boys wouldn't have shoved her. They said they didn't." He shook his head again.

"Go on," John said. It seemed like the man had more to say, and if he was talking, John figured, that was a good thing.

"Guess we'll be late for church now," Halstrom said. He paused for a minute and then said, "I guess there's no reason you shouldn't know what happened with Richard on Friday afternoon, after the hearing."

"What happened?"

"I was hot under the collar after court on Friday. I wasn't angry at the judge or any of you. I was more angry with that other attorney, whatever his name was. Anyway, Jane and I drove separately, so I took off in my truck, and before I got all the way home, I stopped at an old settler's house out there." He jerked his head in a direction beyond the backyard, suggesting someplace even more remote than this one.

Halstrom went on. "Richard was out front. I knew he was squatting there; only Mary and I knew that. I told him we were going to have a come-to-Jesus moment, him and me."

"Why?" John asked.

"He'd been to our place a few weeks before and ever since, Mary wasn't right. So I was going to find out why."

Now John was alert. Maybe Halstrom was going to give him something they could use.

"He kept yelling at me to get off his property and all that, but I ignored him. And I had my Colt 9mm on me, and he knows I'm a good shot. He was saying how much of a bitch Mary is, and I told him he wasn't much of a brother—just a drug-dealing, poor-mouthed, disrespectful worm of a man. But he kept playing like he didn't do anything. Making excuses, but I knew better. He claimed he just asked her for money, because he owed money to some of the boys around here—you know what I mean. Kept saying she's his only kin, so she owes him."

"What else?" John asked.

"Richard said he was putting things back together, moving away. I said fine by me, but what else did he say to Mary that made her not able to speak or function since then? Mr. Quint"—here Halstrom looked straight into John's eyes—"you can't blame me for not just standing by and watching."

John nodded, saying nothing.

"He said he didn't do anything but tell her what was going on: nothing different, just the same old stuff he's into. 'What about the kids?' I asked him. 'Did you talk to them, do anything with them?' He said he just said hello. Then he said the older boy yelled at him, so he smacked him good to teach him a lesson. But what really pissed me off was when he said I'd better raise that kid right or he'd turn into a drug dealer just like the rest of folks around here. So I shot him in the right calf."

"You shot him?"

Halstrom shrugged. "Just a graze," he said. "He had it coming. I told him to get out of town or I'd kill him. Then I got into my truck and left. Like I said, he's gone now. Look: I'm telling you the whole truth here. Richard is terrible, but he's not a liar. I know that. He didn't hurt Amy Jo. Nobody hurt her. You need to get to the bottom of this. I mean it. Fact is, my family is in your hands—yours and the two others inside there and that judge. I have to trust you. That's where I am now."

John thanked Charles for his candor, and they shook hands. There was going to be a lot to share with Cameron and Lara on the ride back to the city.

Chapter 31

THE SHRINK

The day before, Cameron had arranged for a psychologist to meet with Mary Halstrom, and the meeting was scheduled for the following Monday afternoon. Mr. Halstrom would be off from work and available to take her to the doctor's office. An appointment that quick was unusual for any type of medical attention within the child welfare system, especially with Kathryn Camp, who held a PhD in psychology and social work. Cameron had pulled some strings to get the appointment.

The two had worked together on multiple cases before. Cameron brought Dr. Camp up to speed with the Halstroms' situation. She knew that Dr. Camp was a big believer in family unity and regarded out-of-home care akin to a prison sentence, with little chance of psychological recovery.

In the car, coming back from the Halstroms' on Sunday, Cameron told John and Lara about the upcoming appointment. Then she turned to John and said, "Well, how did it go with Charles?"

"It went fine," John said.

"And?"

"Not all that much, really," John said. "I can fill you in a bit later."

In the front seat, Cameron and Lara exchanged looks. Cameron raised her eyebrows, hoping she was conveying that John could be moody sometimes. It looked like Lara understood.

"Okay, later then," Cameron said.

"Yeah, later," John replied.

Lara dropped Cameron off first. The plan was that John would pick them both up in a few hours and head over to the Rays game. Cameron thought she'd rest up before then, maybe even take a nap.

To her surprise, John showed up at her door. He must have gotten in his car and driven over right after Lara dropped him off.

"Let's talk," he said when Cameron let him in.

"Okay," she said. They both sat down in the living room/kitchen.

"Cam, Charles Halstrom has an angry streak. He said he shot his brother-in-law—that it was really just a graze against his leg, no real injury."

"What?"

"You heard me." John described what Halstrom had told him. "I didn't want to get into this in front of Lara. She's new to all of this. I thought you and me should hash it out first."

"That was smart," Cameron agreed. "So, what now?"

"Well—I don't think this means we have to keep Amy Jo in shelter. If anything, it demonstrates that Charles will go to great lengths to protect his family. It doesn't establish child abuse or disprove it. And Richard, the brother-in-law, is a dope dealer. That would reasonably provoke anger."

"Yeah, that seems reasonable," Cameron said. "I buy that. But I'm concerned about the gun. I doubt the judge will like the use of a gun against a family member. That's not hard to figure."

"But have we ever seen a child sheltered because a parent can be angry or shoot a gun?"

"No, but it doesn't put the issue to bed, either—not a shot against a family member, Jesus!"

John looked thoughtful. After a few moments, he said, "I have an idea. Should we enlist Dr. Camp to interview Charles, too? I think Charles would go for it—that guy is fearless. He already said he would meet with a professional. She could drill down further and get more about gun use, other than for hunting. Like has he ever used any kind of weapon on a human being, other than his wife's brother. That doesn't sound too good, does it?"

Cameron nodded. "No, it doesn't, but the idea is smart. It's not like we can hide this or direct Charles into one of our classes on anger. Judge Crowe will be quick to recognize real risk. I'll talk to Dr. Camp to see if we can set it up."

They hung out at Cameron's until it was time to pick up Lara, mostly reading the Sunday edition of the *Tampa Bay Times*.

They picked up Lara and were off to the baseball game. Daniel and Nick were already in their seats, facing the third-base line, midway up the stands, behind the visiting team's dugout. John walked up to them and said, "Hi, guys. You see, I brought the fun ones," as Cameron and Lara followed behind. John wasn't going to screw up this time. This was his kind of place for fun, and he wasn't about to get on Cameron's bad side by crawling into a solitary hole. He volunteered to get some beers and hot dogs.

Lara grabbed a seat between Daniel and Nick. Cameron sat next to Nick, with one remaining seat next to her for John. When he returned, he handed out the food and beers and happily grabbed his seat next to Cameron. The game started.

John provided colorful commentary on the players and team strategies. Nick was a baseball aficionado too, so the two entertained the group as a whole. Cameron, of course, sitting between Nick and John, was in the cross fire of their continuing repartee. She thought it was hilarious. She loved it. At one point, Daniel and Lara fought to catch an errant fly ball headed right for them, but a spectator behind reached over and stole their thunder. They all talked about that the rest of the day.

Chapter 32

INTERROGATION

S triker, day or night, was never in the open for all to see. Other than his typical day-to-day discontent with the world, he never felt out of sorts; he kept his focus on his cool. He did wonder where Sandra was. He figured she'd be out for a few days, no more.

Like most people intent on enjoying a leisurely summer Sunday, he was in the backyard of his hangout, the drug house. He was dressed as usual, in beat-up jeans and a T-shirt, neither particularly clean. It didn't look as though his clothes had been washed since his visit to Alisha's apartment the week before. He had on a pair of sneakers—not barefoot, like he often was—and he had a stubby beard. His black hair with bits of gray was cut close to the scalp. Even with the clothes, the dirt, and the smell, he nevertheless projected a certain charisma. His face was lean, his jaw square, his green eyes deep set and spellbinding in dark-brown skin.

There were others at the house, smoking dope, cooking food, and drinking. All were hot and sweaty. Striker held court, the attendees listening to his social commentary, which they found entertaining.

"You talk about Obama like you trust him and you now feel good, but he's there only a few years, and he's no different from the Man," Striker was saying. "Whatever the color of his skin, his talk is of the capitalist elite. He's still chucking the money to the big defense contractors, his Wall Street brothers, and paying insurance companies big dollars to fatten wallets. It's all a scam."

"Right on, brother," someone said from the crowd.

"Just think about our town," Striker went on. "The filthy rich in isolated places, the working poor scratching to pay bills, police working to keep everyone in line. Don't be suckered into thinking you need to climb on that wagon and reach out for the money hoard. Just enjoy each day, man. Be cool, relax. Work if you want—nothing wrong in that. I respect that, even if you're fattening someone's wallet. But don't buy into it; don't get your mind in the wrong place."

By then everyone was lounging and enjoying the food and drinks. But around 7:00 p.m., things changed. Two cops suddenly came into the backyard, a man and a woman.

"Are you known as Stricker or Striker or Strike?" they asked, coming right up to him.

"Yes, you're right about that," he said.

"What's your real name?" the woman asked.

"Striker."

"How about your birth certificate name?"

"James." Striker was standing with his hands in his back pockets, rocking back and forth nonchalantly. The female officer faced Striker. The other officer looked out at the small crowd of the front yard but asked no questions.

"Your last Christian name?"

"I'm not of religious affiliation, although I'm an admirer of the revolutionary Jesus Christ."

"What name did your mother give you?"

"Didn't have a mother."

"You had a mother."

"True, didn't know a mother. I was a residential burden of the state—not Florida—for at least eighteen years."

"What name did you have in school?"

"Striker. But my report card said James Jefferson."

"Well, Mr. Striker, Mr. Jefferson, let's go to the patrol car. Turn around and let's put on some cuffs."

"Yes, ma'am." He pulled his hands to the front. She touched his back with a gesture to move forward. "No need for direction," Striker said. "I see your patrol car."

At the station, they entered a side door into a small room with one overhead light. Another cop, presumably a detective, was dressed in street clothes. The cuffs were removed.

"Mr. Striker, I'm a detective with the Tampa Police Department. I'm investigating a matter involving Sandra Williams. I assume you know her."

"Well."

"Did you hear your rights from the police officers?"

"Yes."

"Do you know your rights?"

"I do. Been arrested before—never charged. I reserve my right to an attorney, but for now, what's this about?"

"You know I get to ask the questions. This is about Sandra Williams."

"Yes, sir. How is she?"

"Well, what do you think?"

"I assume she's fine but haven't seen her for days."

"What happened to her?" the detective continued.

"She lost her child to the government. Not a good thing."

"Yes, we know that."

"All right," Striker said. "What else happened to her? Where is she?"

"Like I said, I get to ask the questions."

"Look, I don't know why I'm here. If you know something about me or Sandra that I don't know, I suggest you tell me. Otherwise, I'm not talking anymore. And I want a lawyer."

At that, the detective walked out. Striker was left in the holding cell until midnight and then released with no explanation. They asked for an address and phone number, but since he had none, he agreed to check in every few days with the police. He was given cards with phone numbers from the two police officer friends of John.

He left into the night, with one thought: Where was Sandra, and was she okay?

Chapter 33

NURSE RATCHED

John was full of himself Monday morning, having enjoyed the ball game so much on Sunday. He'd enjoyed talking baseball statistics, trivia, and strategy with everyone.

It was going to be a full day: going to court with Cameron in the Halstrom case before Judge Crowe in the early afternoon, checking in with Sandra at the hospital, maybe conducting more useless groundwork on the whereabouts of Jack Wilson, and following up on Juan Martinez. The ball game had been a good release for him. He felt pumped.

"Morning, Cam," he said when he arrived at the office. "Yesterday was fun. Great ball game."

"It was fun!" she said. "And you really know baseball. Good for you, champ. So today, listen up: I've got to get my thoughts together on Halstrom. I need to make sure the mother shows up at Dr. Camp's office. I'm not sure how to handle the shooting issue with Charles Halstrom. Maybe just play that by ear, let the waters settle before I bring it up with Judge Crowe? What do you think?" She wrote some notes to herself. John watched her but didn't respond.

"What do you mean exactly?" he asked.

"I mean I'll go over the strong points first, in favor of releasing Amy Jo from shelter. Get the judge convinced on the front end and then go over the shooting. Maybe the judge will look past it and think strictly of the best interests of Amy Jo with a mostly good family."

"That's risky, but you make a good point. Let's do it that way."

"Okay."

"I'll join you at the Halstrom hearing this afternoon, if that's no problem with you," John said. "The judge will be happy about the psych consult with Dr. Camp, but something seems to be keeping her from reuniting her with the family. It could be anything. You need to think about that. I'm going to check in on Sandra Williams now. Catch you this afternoon."

"Thanks. And we'd better get back to the Santeroa and Williams cases at some point, too."

"I know," John said. "First things first, okay?"

John reached the hospital at about 10:00 a.m., walked up to Sandra's room, and peeked in. Sandra wasn't there. He checked with the nurses' station, and they told him that she'd been discharged on Sunday.

"What?" he exclaimed. "Sorry, but how could she possibly be discharged? She was almost in a coma last week, and now she's discharged?"

"Well, sir, you need to speak with the doctor. She's not here right now. Ms. Williams did great; she was fully cognitive. The hospital can't keep people when they're well. Please check with the doctor. That's about all we can tell you. You're not a relative or caregiver."

"All right," he said, thinking he had finally encountered a real Nurse Ratched. "But where did she go?"

"She was picked up by the hospital's social worker. I assume she went home."

John left and immediately called Cameron. She answered from her office line, still working to prepare for the afternoon.

"They discharged Sandra. Can you believe that? She's probably headed home, and that can't be safe. The perp is still out there somewhere."

"You have to get over to her apartment," Cameron said, with urgency in her voice. "This is a major screwup. My God, are those hospital people crazy?"

"We're not family. I got that lecture from Nurse Ratched."

"Who?" Cameron asked.

"Never mind," John said. "Okay, just so you're not left hanging, Ratched was a mean nurse to a mental patient played by Jack Nicholson in *One Flew over the Cuckoo's Nest*. It's a movie from 1975."

"Glad you know your trivia," Cameron said, laughing.

John got to Sandra's apartment and knocked on the door. She was still bruised but obviously up and able to get around. She looked tired.

"Thanks for coming over. I should have called you. They discharged me, and I'm glad to be feeling okay, but I miss David."

She started to cry, and John stood silent, wishing Cameron were with him. Then he sat down and dropped his forehead into his hands. He hoped Sandra wouldn't get hysterical. But where was the perp?

Sandra pulled herself up into a slouch. She told him that her neighbors, Delores Reed and her husband, had cooked her dinner the night before and visited her this morning.

"I know you want me to remember who beat me, but I don't," she said. "That's why you're here, right? But can you help me with David?"

"I'll help as much as I can, but it'll take some time. Right now, I need to get you into a safe place, maybe arrange for some type of protection. We can take you to see David; you have unsupervised visitation rights, so that's no problem. But maybe you need to calm down before we go over there. I know this is hard, and I know you're a good mother. Things'll work out, with a little time. Are you all right?"

"I'll get it together. I'm scared. I've never really been scared before. I did stick to my case plan."

"Sandra, I'm on your side, but with what happened to you here, we have to get you to some other place. Otherwise, I'm not sure what the court will do, or what the state's deputy attorney will say. Do you understand? I'll hang out here for a couple of hours. I can do work over my phone. Maybe you should just get some rest. Do you want something to drink or eat?"

Sandra shook her head. "I'll be okay. Maybe you better tell the Reeds you're here."

John stepped out of the apartment and went over to the Reeds, who were happy to see him. Mrs. Reed wanted to talk, but he begged off. He said he'd talk to them before he left. Back in Sandra's apartment, she was watching TV. He called Cameron from the kitchen to say that he doubted he would make it to court.

He sat outside on the steps. He was getting nowhere with Sandra. He believed her when she said that she couldn't remember. She'd said nothing about Jack Wilson, good or bad, and what about Striker? She knew him, but he didn't seem to cross her mind enough to mention him.

He called his cop friends, and they told him that they had picked up Striker yesterday. But they got no information out of him, so they let him go. The detective said he wasn't sure Striker even knew about Sandra's condition. Apparently, Striker had agreed to check in with the police every so often, which they thought was unusual. They also somehow believed that he'd keep his word.

John asked if they could drop by Sandra's apartment to check on things and discuss the situation with him. They agreed and promised to be there after they made rounds, unless there was some emergency.

"No emergency," John said. He hoped that was true.

Chapter 34

ORDER IN THE COURT

Judge Crowe convened court Monday afternoon, at 1:30 p.m. sharp. She had already heard fifteen cases that morning. The clerk called the Halstrom case, and the judge took appearances, including Charles Halstrom. Then she addressed Cameron.

"Well, Ms. Springer, how was your weekend?"

"Morning, your honor. It was nice, thank you. I do have more to report today."

"Good. I gave some thought to this case over the weekend and picked up the file to study the record, which at this point is meager at best. We left three young boys with the parents and left a three-year-old sister in shelter, based, I assume, on a child battery opinion of an emergency physician. I've heard no testimony from the physician, just statements from you, the caseworker, the father and aunt, and arguments from two lawyers—all getting us nowhere. It seems you, the guardian ad litem, and her attorney want the child moved back home. I have concerns about the three boys left behind. I can't get my mind around this.

No one has given me any information on how the three-year-old was injured. And in another case, where I did support the removal of a child, I have since learned that the mother was beaten up and put in the hospital. I don't know who did it or her current condition."

"Understood, your honor." Cameron stood up to address the judge. "The guardian ad litem, Lara Liu; my superior, John Quint; and I visited the Halstrom home on Saturday and Sunday mornings. We found the three boys to be in good care. They were roughhousing Saturday morning, and on Sunday they were getting ready for church. They play pretty hard with each other, spend a lot of time outdoors, but it all seems good-natured. I think Mr. Halstrom already testified about some broken bones from horseback riding. Mr. Halstrom does appear to exercise thoughtful and respectful oversight, which the boys follow. There are alligators nearby that crawl to the side of the road for sun, but Mr. Halstrom and the boys appear to exercise due care. The home is in good order. I do have to say that their mother, Mary Halstrom, continues in the same condition we encountered last week: uncommunicative and withdrawn. Mr. Halstrom agreed for his wife to see Dr. Camp this evening and for him to meet with her as well. I believe your honor is familiar with Dr. Camp?"

"Yes, I know Dr. Camp."

"So the point of the meeting with Dr. Camp is to assist Mrs. Halstrom strictly from a medical standpoint and, of course, if appropriate, to determine any social assistance that might be helpful from a parenting standpoint."

Judge Crowe perked up at this. "Well, so long as Mr. Halstrom is in agreement. The ultimate purpose of this proceeding is the welfare of the four children. I assume you understand that, Ms. Springer."

"I do, Judge, but with Dr. Camp there might be some carryover or adjustments as to our assessment of the home."

"All right, I accept that so long as Mr. Halstrom does. Mr. Halstrom, is that agreeable?"

"Yes, ma'am, thank you."

Cameron looked down at her notes briefly. "Oh, yes, Judge, there is another point to address before we close this hearing. But before we do that, we need some access to medical records, quickly. We need a court order to that effect. Otherwise, we may experience more delay. Ms. Liu plans to establish a line of communication with counsel for the hospital this afternoon. At this point, with regard to the hospital report of suspected child abuse, we don't really know the basis for that report—there may or may not be any basis. And that may lead to an interview of the child—she is three years old and can talk at that level—by the court or maybe a child social worker or psychologist."

"Let's first interview the hospital personnel and review the medical records," Judge Crowe said. "At this point we've sheltered a child based on nothing but an injury, some hearsay, and maybe some speculation about Mrs. Halstrom. You did multiple home inspections during which you've observed a healthy environment, except maybe for the alligators. Mr. Halstrom, what about the alligators?" At this point, Cameron took her seat.

Mr. Halstrom stood up. "Judge, I've never had any problems. They don't really come on our property. We don't have any dogs or cats—nothing to tempt them. I've lived among them my whole life—snakes, gators, hawks, even panthers. We're safe."

"How far away are the gators?"

"They sun in the winter about a hundred yards down the road. In the summer they're mostly in the swamp water; might come out a little but mostly stay close to the water."

"Thank you, Mr. Halstrom. Let's all be mindful of the environmental and animal conditions and make sure they don't become an issue,

Ms. Springer. Please submit to me today a form of order for medical records this afternoon, and let's get this done quickly. Does the deputy attorney general have any objections, Mr. Stalnick?"

He jumped at the invitation. "Judge, are we really going to permit these boys to remain with their father and mother? At the last hearing, we established that Mr. Halstrom beat the boys—well, spanked them, even testified about a switch. We know they've suffered broken bones. This is a neglectful home."

With that, Cameron looked up from her notes and reached for her armrest, ready to jump up. Lara touched her hand firmly to hold Cameron back, so she remained in her seat. Halstrom bolted from his chair. Judge Crowe quickly motioned for him to sit. "Hold on there, Mr. Halstrom. I understand the attorney's words are provocative, but don't make this situation worse."

He sat down but slowly, with a steely glare at Stalnick. The bailiff approached Mr. Halstrom's side. Judge Crowe remained calm. Stalnick looked over his shoulder at Halstrom. "Nothing further," he said.

Judge Crowe took charge. "Everyone, I expect order in this courtroom, without exception. Now, Ms. Springer, what is this other matter you wish to bring before the court? Time's running short."

"Judge, yesterday, my supervisor, Mr. Quint, interviewed Mr. Halstrom in depth. This was an exercise of due caution, to expose any other matters of concern. During this process, as recollected by Mr. Quint, Mr. Halstrom said that last week, when Amy Jo was in shelter, Mr. Halstrom had an altercation with his wife's brother, Richard."

Judge Crowe interrupted Cameron. "Where is Mr. Quint? Shouldn't he give this to me firsthand rather than as hearsay?"

"Your honor, he did plan to be here, but this morning he learned that Sandra Williams, the victim of the beating last Thursday morning, was discharged by the hospital and was back at her apartment where she was beaten. So he's over there now, working to get her out of the apartment into safe housing."

"Thank you for that explanation. Good for Mr. Quint. Continue. What about the altercation?"

"Judge, Mr. Halstrom argued with Richard—not at Mr. Halstrom's house or property but at an abandoned settler's house a number of miles away, down an otherwise-inaccessible dirt road."

Mr. Halstrom stood up again.

"Mr. Halstrom, sit back down," Judge Crowe said. "At this point, do not comment on any of this. I'm not sure where this is going. Continue, Ms. Springer."

"Mr. Halstrom objected to Richard's drug dealing and learned that Richard had hit Mr. Halstrom's eldest son, who was in some way defending his mother. During this altercation, Mr. Halstrom gave some warnings and fired revolver shots into the ground where Richard stood, and possibly one shot grazed his leg. Richard said he was leaving town for good and felt sorry for his sister."

Mr. Stalnick stood up. "Judge, see what I mean?"

"You, too, Mr. Stalnick: sit down until you are called on. Ms. Springer, are you through? Mr. Halstrom, under these circumstances, do not comment in any way on Ms. Springer's statement. Only one simple question: Are you willing to meet with Dr. Camp this evening?"

"Yes, ma'am."

"Mr. Burt, does the guardian, Ms. Liu, have a position on this?"

"Yes, your honor. Having visited the Halstrom home two times to observe the family, the guardian agrees with the position of Ms. Springer and welcomes the involvement of Dr. Camp."

"Ms. Springer, I assume you will consult with the state's attorney, criminal division, on those revelations. In the meantime, the state will continue to shelter Amy Jo Halstrom until at least our next hearing.

Day-to-day visits by Ms. Springer and Ms. Liu at the Halstrom home shall continue tomorrow and thereafter until ordered otherwise. Mr. Halstrom, make sure you exercise good control over the boys, and I think you know what I mean. Let's not have any broken bones falling off a horse or, for that matter, a chair. Ms. Jane Halstrom, can you make arrangements to be at the house during the next few days as we run down some more information?"

Jane nodded, and the judge continued. "And, Ms. Springer, try to get a report from Dr. Camp this evening and, if necessary or appropriate, take action in due course."

"Yes," Cameron said, "happy to."

"All right. Let's get back here on Wednesday of this week. Madam clerk, please schedule a hearing."

"Yes, Judge," she said, "10:00 a.m. Wednesday, this week."

Mr. Stalnick stepped out into the lobby, and Chad Burt followed him. Cameron wondered what the two would have to say to each other.

At the elevator, Chad Burt caught up to Stalnick and said, "Let's have a talk."

"Fine," Stalnick replied with a surly tone, placing his hands on his hips. "Are you sure you want to be connected with this mess?"

"Listen up, Stalnick: What's the problem here? Cameron and Lara are working this case hard, using their best judgment, and you keep hitting them with negativity. Maybe you should stick around and learn the facts before popping off and giving them a hard time."

"Really, Chad, you mean that?" Stalnick retorted, staring at Burt. "What gives you the right to dress me down?"

"Get yourself under control. And who have you talked to about the Halstroms? Your own caseworker is working to look after this family, and you have yet to sit down and get the facts. You're working for yourself, not your client."

"I don't always listen to the caseworkers," Stalnick said. "What do they really know? These cases usually twist against the children, and then we're caught up in a firestorm, with plenty of bad press. Anyway, you work one case at a time. I'm over here all day listening to this stuff."

"Look," said Burt, lifting his hands in exasperation, "let's try to get along. I'm pointing out that Cameron could use some good support from you as opposed to you throwing her under the bus."

"Chad, you made your points, and they are duly noted. Let's see what happens to these kids."

"Yeah, like foster or residential care. We know how bad that is. Not a good track record there."

"You've said your piece. We'll have to deal with this again—sooner rather than later. And I hope nothing happens," Stalnick said, walking off. Chad found Cameron and Lara, who had been watching them argue.

Chad said, "You're not going to get the state on your side on this one. You might be the expert in the trenches, but he doesn't seem to care. He's marching to his own drum. This isn't good, but I want you to keep it up. I'm with the two of you. Let's see what Dr. Camp says."

"Thanks," said Cameron. "For a minute there, I was thinking you and Stalnick were about to punch each other. Now that would be fitting in this case, as crazy as it seems."

Lara asked Cameron to follow her to her office, saying, "You can crash there for a bit and stare out at the bay with a nice, cold glass of water, not beer!"

At Lara's office, Cameron called John to bring him up to date and was relieved to hear that he'd found a Catholic charity program to house Sandra Williams that evening. He'd helped her pack up a few things to get her out of the apartment as soon as possible. *Thank God*, Cameron thought to herself, exhausted from the day's events. At least something was going right.

Chapter 35

AGITATED

True to form, Striker strolled around the neighborhood in the cool of Monday evening. *Cool* was relative, of course; it just meant a drop from the high nineties to maybe the high eighties. There had been the typical late-afternoon tropical downpour, dropping the temperature but not the humidity. Striker didn't mind the heat or the steaminess. He'd lived long enough in Tampa to become accustomed to it. His jeans sagged from the wet air, and his shirt stuck to his skin as if he'd been dunked in a tank. Wet and salty. He liked it.

Escaping the downpour by ducking into the drug house, he figured he might sleep there or in some vacant building nearby. After the rain, he walked a couple of blocks in the vaguely cooler air. No one was at the drug house. Maybe he'd run into Sandra. That would make him feel better. Her absence and the presence of the police had made him uneasy.

Suddenly, Jack Wilson jumped out of the bushes. The dusk was heavy, almost dark now.

"What the fuck," Striker yelled as he jumped back toward the street. "Again? Are you a child or what? Next time I won't hold back, and you'll get hit."

"Cool it, Striker. I told you I was lying low. I was out on my bike when the sun started to go down. Got soaked. It's hot and miserable." Wilson looked better than he did the other day: this time he was relatively clean, wearing a collared shirt, and he had a belt on—his pants weren't hanging off his hips. His black hair was combed and in place, even in the rain.

"Never seen you on a bike, and you look decent," Striker observed. "And that's hardly lying low. At night you stick out with that white skin of yours." Striker was walking slowly, looking comfortable and at ease. He had shoes on—a shoddy pair of sneakers.

Wilson smirked at him. "Okay, my man. Funny coming from you, a mixed breed. Look, I got the bike just for today. I had to get out of my safe house. No need to talk particulars."

"I don't know what you mean. But for some reason I don't see you around unless you're jumping out of bushes." Striker often thought Wilson was somewhat of a basket case emotionally—he projected toughness but inside was kind of a wimp. Sandra was good for him, even though Striker thought she was way too tolerant.

"Don't go gettin' all inquisitive on me," Wilson said. "I just biked over to Bayshore, hung around the seawall. Some nice-looking females out there. Listen, I'm going to get some food. Something's going on: the police are on the streets all the time. You seen 'em?"

"I got picked up yesterday," Striker admitted. "They asked me a bunch of questions about Sandra. They let me go around about midnight."

Wilson suddenly looked alert. "What about Sandra? What'd they want to know?"

"They wanted to know what happened to her. I told them she lost her son to the state; I mean, we all know that. Nothing else."

"That's right. Good reason to lie low."

Striker looked at him hard. "You have something to say to me?"

"Listen, I'm outta here, back to my house. I don't trust the police."

Striker raised his hand and pointed at Wilson. "Get your shit together," he said. "Don't be crawling around in bushes. Where's this house of yours, and do you know where Sandra is?"

Wilson only said, "See you. I've gotta do what I gotta do. Check you later. And don't ask me anything."

Wilson slipped back behind the bushes and in an instant was gone. Striker couldn't believe how quickly Wilson had made off. It was just an empty lot of palmettos and palms, thick with deep green vegetation, like a swamp, and pitch-dark. Touching his lips with his fingers, Striker stared at the palmettos and wondered what the fuck was going on. Nothing seemed right. He felt agitated. Maybe he should go underground, too. He never should have gone to the house the other day, especially with the cops showing up. What was that all about? And where was he going to go now?

He walked another block or so, turned around, walked some more, and then he stopped. Finally, he looked up and said, "Shit." He had nowhere to go. All he could do was keep walking. Maybe he would figure out where Sandra was.

He covered all of East Tampa, from the docks to the University of South Florida and everything between, including Seminole Heights, Suitcase City, and the Hillsborough River flowing into Tampa Bay from the swamps and wetlands. By early morning, he was exhausted, wet, and stinking hot. He didn't know what else to do, but it was clear to him that he was being drawn to Sandra's.

It was around 5:00 in the morning when he got there. The apartment was dark, the door open. Things were crashing about. A chair flew out the door, a window smashed, and a man was screaming, "Whore bitch, motherfucker!" Striker hid behind trees across the street.

Eventually, the crashing stopped. A masked figure ran out of the apartment, down the stairs, and into the early morning. Striker didn't recognize the guy. Then sirens sounded, and police showed up. It was the two cops Striker had seen patrolling the area earlier.

The cops ran upstairs and met an elderly woman from the next-door apartment. He'd seen her before, the lady with the disabled husband: nice but talkative, a busybody.

Striker didn't move until the cops left, not wanting to present them with any opportunities. He'd promised to check in with them. Now what was he going to do? Talking to cops wasn't his style. And where was Sandra?

Chapter 36

PSYCHOANALYSIS

Monday evening, while Striker was wandering around Tampa, Cameron got a call from Dr. Camp. Cameron was still in her office, anxiously awaiting the call.

"So you met with Mary and Charles Halstrom," Cameron said. "What did you find out?"

"Yes, I have news," Dr. Camp said. "But let's talk about it at Bern's. We can sit in the bar and have a drink and a steak sandwich. What do you say?"

Bern's was a steak house, with supposedly the world's largest restaurant wine cellar. It was where a lot of people met up to talk shop and was also always jam-packed with tourists, so Cameron knew there would be no problem with them being seen there together. For a second, she wondered if she could afford it but decided to overlook her budget for once. "I've never been there," she admitted. "But let's do it. See you there in about thirty minutes." She stopped by her apartment to spruce up and change. She wasn't about to go to Bern's looking like the broke social worker she was.

They had to wait a few minutes before a table opened up. Once they were seated, Cameron got down to business. "Should I ask you questions, or do you prefer to give me an oral report?"

Dr. Camp, a stylish woman in her mid-forties with brown hair, was in good spirits. She had a glass of cold sauvignon blanc to start the evening. Cameron did likewise, following her lead. Dr. Camp said, "Basically, I find no long-term, chronic psychological condition or behavioral or personality trait in Mary Halstrom that might impede her parenting skills or negatively affect her ability to serve as a mother to Amy Jo or her siblings. But she is depressed, significantly, and it's been brought on, most likely, by the behavior of her brother, Richard, and his related problems. This is her first experience with this condition. There's no evidence of suicidal ideation and no evidence of any aggressive or physical behavior. Other than the way she hangs her head and looks down all the time, there are no physical manifestations of mental illness: no habitual gestures, no knee bouncing. I will say that I do find it odd that she's gone over the cliff because of this brother. For some reason, it must be very sensitive for her to address. I bet it's buried down deep in the subconscious, probably back to early childhood. Somehow, after all these years, she still hasn't developed an emotional defense to her brother's behavior."

Cameron listened intently. "Okay, that's good to hear—I mean the part about Richard and her sensitivity to him. It's troublesome, but also that's how life is sometimes, just very hard." She frowned. "That's kind of simplistic to say; sorry," she said.

"No, you're right, Cam. Life is hard."

"Are you sure about this, after one session? Are we missing anything?

That's my fear in this case. Because frankly, at this point, I can't see any reason to continue to shelter Amy Jo from her parents and family."

"Believe it or not, she kind of opened up," Dr. Camp said. "Not totally, but enough for me to get a workable picture. And I know her history from her husband."

"I have to confess that he's a likable guy, but is he pulling the wool over our eyes?" Cameron asked. "I just can't decide. What'd you think?"

"I think he's the genuine article. What you see is what you get. I spent a total of four hours between the two of them. I think they're more or less a healthy family, not the destructive stuff I see every day. It's almost like a case study for me." Dr. Camp said this happily. She even seemed refreshed by the experience. "It's nice to encounter a healthy family—the cowboy and the depressed wife, sure, but still different and nice."

"Okay, but what do you think about Charles Halstrom shooting the brother-in-law?" Cameron raised her eyebrows and drew her hands to the back of her head. "What about that?"

Dr. Camp nodded. "Yes, he grazed Richard with one shot. But I think it was a reaction to a threat to his family. He confirmed that Richard had been a lifelong drain on Mary financially and, most importantly, emotionally. She loves her brother and has always supported him. For what it's worth, Charles thinks Richard will be gone at least for some time, but there are no guarantees. And there's no evidence of serious mistreatment with the children. He did spank the kids, yes. But Mary is basically a sweet and mild woman, probably loving to a fault."

The waiter arrived with food. They split a large New York strip steak, medium rare, with two more glasses of wine, this time a pricey Bordeaux.

Cameron was out of her element and transfixed by the joy of it all. She was beginning to appreciate the way they were constructively dealing with a difficult family issue, based on the light at the end of the tunnel turned on by Dr. Camp.

Dr. Camp looked Cameron in the eye and said, "I don't have any information on how Amy Jo broke her shoulder. But based on my analysis, it wasn't because of Charles or Mary Halstrom."

Chapter 37

BLACK DIRT AND ROCKS

Early Tuesday morning, Lara Liu drove to meet with in-house counsel for the hospital, together with the emergency care doctor who had attended Amy Jo's broken shoulder. Afterward, she called Cameron to fill her in.

"I had a good meeting with Dr. Camp last night," Cameron told her. "We had dinner at Bern's. Definitely better than bean soup and Cubans with John, even if it wasn't cheap. What did the hospital and doctor have to say?"

"I'm glad there was some fun in it," Lara said. "Completely different from my experience at the hospital."

"What do you mean?" Cameron asked.

"It was pretty formal. The hospital attorney showed up. I handed her a copy of the court order and subpoena. She turned over the hospital's file on the emergency care treatment. I swear the documents were over one inch thick."

"Seriously? You've got to be kiddin' me. That's hilarious: one big thick file. I can't believe it."

"Absolutely," Lara said, and they both laughed before Lara went on. "The admission documents stated the usual: time of admission, admitting doctor, reason for admission. The 'sore and bruised shoulder.' The attending physician made notes. According to her notes, Amy Jo's father was helpful, and Amy Jo seemed comfortable and snuggled in his arms. There was no bruising on any part of the body other than the top-right part of the shoulder. The physician removed Amy Jo's shirt for an upper body examination. The right shoulder portion of the shirt was particularly dirty with—and I'm quoting here—'engrained black dirt and some very small rock particles.' The documents reported that Mr. Halstrom said it was the same shirt she wore on the afternoon of the accident. He was afraid to take off the shirt for fear of hurting her. He had asked her how the injury occurred, and she said she fell, or at least he said that's what he understood she said. He said at the time she was in pain and crying, so he wasn't exactly sure. Mr. Halstrom offered no other explanation for the injury. Based on his failure to explain, the physician had noted 'suspicious for nonaccidental injury,' which prompted her to call the state's child abuse hotline."

"That all checks out so far," Cameron said. "Go on."

"There were also diagnostic tests, including radiology reports. X-rays were taken, and the radiologist noted there was a hairline fracture of the humerus—the upper arm bone—indicative of some type of blunt trauma. Amy Jo was discharged to the care of the father, and instructions were given for care of the injury."

"So that's it?" Cameron asked.

"Not quite," Lara said. "Once I finished the document review, I called the attorney and asked to speak with the doctor. The doctor confirmed the accuracy of her notes. I asked if she knew Amy Jo had been abused, and she said no. There was just the question about how the shoulder injury occurred. She said Amy Jo gave no concrete explanation about how she was hurt. The doctor placed a call to the hotline because it was standard procedure for an unexplained injury to a child. I asked about the presence of the dirt and engrained rocks, as noted on the shirt, whether that could represent a fall. The physician said sure. I asked her if she was aware that the Halstroms' house was surrounded by grass, dirt, and rocks. She said she didn't know that."

"So what you're saying is that the doctor has no opinion as to whether there was any child abuse?" Cameron asked.

"Right," Lara said. "She just speculated that maybe there was because there was no definitive explanation for the injury. The hospital records state that the child said she fell."

"I thought the hospital reported child abuse to the hotline. Isn't that what we were told?"

"I don't know that. I wasn't around early on," Lara said.

"That's right. Sorry. I think we learned that from the deputy sheriffs. What exactly did they tell me? I know they told me about the hotline. I'm not sure what else. We got handed the case from the sheriffs. I'm not at all sure what the hotline reported. You've always got to pay attention to the small stuff. Let me think a minute."

Finally, from the other end of the line, Cameron heard Lara take in a breath. "Look, Cam, as far as we know, Amy Jo fell off a tricycle or ran into a pile of rocks and dirt or, most likely, fell off something like a ladder out in the yard. I mean, that would be logical, and we've both seen the place. Maybe some outside force was present, but it's hard to know. And, again, for what it's worth, the reports, such as they were, noted that Amy Jo said she fell."

"Well, good work, Lara," Cameron said. "I wish we worked together all the time! We have another hearing before Judge Crowe tomorrow morning. I think we'll be in good shape by then. Do you have copies of the medical records?"

"Right here, next to me in my car."

"Good. You wouldn't believe what John and I have been through. Sandra Williams was out of the hospital and back in her apartment with no protection. John had to move her to a safe place. I'll fill you in on the details later."

"You'd better," Lara said.

Cameron smiled. "Let's meet at the courthouse tomorrow morning at 9:00. Try to have Chad there. And, Lara—thanks for everything. I mean it."

"No problem," Lara said. "See you then."

Cameron hung up her phone, thinking about what she'd just learned. She thought that, at best, the hospital records were inconclusive and, at worst, were suggestive of only a simple fall.

Chapter 38

BACK TO THE UNION HALL

Ten minutes after Cameron had spoken with Lara, John got a call from his two cop friends. They told him about the intrusion and destruction of Sandra's apartment. Apparently, Mrs. Reed, the neighbor, had stepped outside to see what the commotion was and got a quick look at the intruder, but he wore a mask.

John immediately called the Catholic charity to ensure that Sandra was all right. She was, and he told her to stay inside and that he'd come over and talk with her in person to explain.

Cameron, eavesdropping from her cubicle, bounced around the corner and demanded an update. John told her what was going on with Sandra.

"I'm going to go talk to her right now," he said.

"Something's going on here," Cameron said. "This sounds like a stalker with malicious intent." What was the motivation? Did Sandra have some kind of secret life they didn't know about? Leaving David alone to venture out of the apartment onto a balcony was one thing, but when confronted, Sandra had genuinely seemed contrite, and she'd been honest about her trouble with the bus system during her search for a job.

Now Cameron felt fear—fear for Sandra and David Williams, for Alisha and Elijah Santeroa, and maybe for herself as well. "I need to think about this," she said to John.

"Take your time," he said.

Cameron's mind began to work. Sandra's beating, the trashing of her apartment, John moving her to safe quarters—something was missing. She'd met both Sandra and Alisha and had read the case files, and by now she'd met numerous people to discuss the situation, but was there something about Alisha or Sandra that was vulnerable? Did Patricia, the caseworker on vacation, have some inside information? The case files revealed nothing, as far as Cameron recalled. Maybe she should review them again.

Finally, Cameron peered around her cubicle at John. "So someone is stalking Sandra, and for what reason? I get that the police are working on this, but is David in the crosshairs? Did the police ask you any questions?"

"Not yet," John told her. "They gave me a heads-up about the break-in. These were the cops I worked with on Alisha's case, the same ones who showed up the night Sandra was beaten. The police picked up the Striker guy on Sunday but got nothing out of him. I don't know."

"I'm going to try to get a hold of Patricia and dig into the case files again," Cameron said.

"Good. Let's not just sit back and wait on the police," John said. "I'm not sure what I should be doing. Getting out on the street right now doesn't seem too smart. I've come up with nothing except that I'm scared out of my mind at the prospect of a strange man jumping out of the bushes again."

"Are you really? I doubt it, but glad to see you finally admit you're no cop or criminal investigator," Cameron said. "For now, what do you think about getting the lowdown on Juan Martinez and leaving the rest behind? We know very little about him. Maybe you should go down to the union hall again."

John agreed. Meanwhile, Cameron said she'd try to get in touch with Patricia.

———

John wondered about going to the café where he'd gotten the tip about the drug house but brushed it off and ended up at the union hall. He told the receptionist that he worked with Kids Care and somehow worked the necessary magic to get back into the office of a union official.

"Thanks for seeing me," he said. The official sat behind a big desk, with all sorts of awards hanging from the walls.

"Go ahead," the man said.

"This will be a mouthful, but I need you to understand. I have some issues that could benefit from some simple information. This is about a stevedore named Juan Martinez, originally from New York City. I have to check him out. I'm a social worker with Kids Care, and Mr. Martinez has some type of relationship with a mother within our care. All I need to know is that Mr. Martinez is, in fact, a stevedore and that his record at work is good, from your standpoint. This is most likely for his benefit as well. My partner, Cameron Springer, visited with him and had a good impression, so we just need backup. We're not the police, and Mr. Martinez is not in trouble. He just looks after the child now and then."

The official listened, seeming neither intimidated nor suspicious of John. Rising from his seat, he said, "How about you give me a few minutes, and I'll think about it? Have a seat in the lobby."

After fifteen minutes, the official emerged.

"Look, I can't give you any confidential information; I'm sure you know that. But I can tell you that Martinez is a stevedore, a member of the union, and in good standing. We are unaware of any problems. How does that work for you?"

"Thanks," John said. "I think that's all I need. I appreciate your time. And here's my card. Call me anytime."

Back at the office, he gave Cameron his report on his visit. "Well, the guy is employed, at least."

Cameron shook her head. "Look, we just don't know. It's a reference, and I get that one bad experience isn't everything, but I'm still on the fence about Martinez."

"All right, I am too," John said. "I'm not at the point of giving the guy a total pass just yet."

Cameron turned in her chair and opened FinCen to find the files on Alisha. Even though she'd pored over the records a few days earlier, she wanted to check again. She turned again to the most interesting case note, the one she'd read a few days before: *Alisha is a bright and inquisitive young lady.* . . . Nothing else jumped out to her, and everything seemed to check out—yet she wondered whether Alisha was holding anything back.

She opened her phone and checked her texts—just work stuff. Maybe it was a good night to have a few drinks and a little fun and then get to court first thing in the morning and maybe wrap up the Halstrom case. She texted Daniel, who replied that he was up for going out and that he'd get Nick to join them. Then she texted Grace, who said she'd be there too. Cameron decided to leave John alone for the evening, needing a real break from work and not wanting a night where she'd have to worry about who was getting along.

Chapter 39

FOUR GLASSES OF WINE

Cameron got to Sam's about 8:00 p.m., after a shower, nap, and quick catch-up on the news. It was just nice to lounge at the apartment for a couple of hours. John didn't call, and she was relieved to not have to talk shop with him just now; they were both exhausted. None of her friends were at the bar yet. Cameron was never on time and had little experience waiting on others, so this was going to be more downtime than she had bargained for. She ordered a glass of sauvignon blanc, like she'd had at Bern's.

Within fifteen minutes, Grace showed up. "I oversaw another concrete pour today," she reported. "And the project's moving along on schedule, which is saying something. Exciting life I have, huh? How about you?" She had rushed into Sam's and charged into a seat next to Cameron, hands flying back and forth. "Forget that," she said. "I haven't talked to you since the other night's call, you know, about Daniel. Anything to report? What about the baseball game?"

"I'm treading water," Cameron said. "Daniel is fine; no problems there. I think maybe that was just about nothing. Time will tell. I had a great time at the ball game, really loads of fun. The real thing is the three cases pushing me. One is particularly bad, a young mother beaten up and now her apartment trashed."

Grace looked concerned. "That's bad. Is she all right? Your job's always interesting. And you're not a quitter; we all know that. But, wow, what's going on?"

"She's okay and in a safe place. In another case, I'm trying to get a little girl back to her family. The father is a legitimate cowboy, which I know sounds strange. And I'm trying to figure out why these cases with two single moms are making me uncomfortable. One minute I'm confident, the next I'm anxious."

"Exciting world you work in."

Cameron shook her head. "There's excitement for sure, but this job is over everyone's head. No one really knows how to assess this stuff. They don't train you, not really. How am I supposed to know if these cases will turn out just fine?"

"You've told me this a million times, and you keep working at it," Grace responded. "Just remember you don't have to be there all your life. You can hang in for a while and then get out. Everyone appreciates what you do."

"You're wrong about that. No one appreciates what we do, or at least it doesn't seem like it."

Nick walked in. "Over here," Cameron called out. "Save us from ourselves!"

Grace rolled her eyes and whispered to Cameron, "Now, there's something to talk about."

"No problem, at your service," Nick said. Grabbing a seat, he gave each woman a hug and a big fat kiss on the cheek. "Now," he said, "what's the problem?"

Grace and Cameron laughed. "What problem?"

Daniel walked in. "I see I'm not needed here. I'll come back tomorrow. You see the Rays lost this afternoon? They were on a roll and look what happens."

"Didn't see it and don't care," Nick said. "We have no problems. That was just established."

"That's right, no problems. I'll have another one of these, please," Cameron said, holding up her empty wineglass.

Nick said he had her covered. Cameron couldn't help liking that. Grace rolled her eyes again.

Cameron hadn't thought about Nick as much recently, she realized. She'd had fun with him at the game, of course, and Nick was a charmer—handsome, with wavy, blond hair, kind of tall, and big shoulders. She still found him attractive, but it didn't feel too intense or distracting. She liked that. Anyway, she didn't want to get into a situation where she might get hurt.

Nick wasn't one to miss an opportunity. "So, looked like you and Grace were into something heavy when I walked in. Anything going on?"

"Just girl talk," Cameron said, laughing. "But I'm not going to say any more." She smiled at Nick, enjoying the appreciative look in his eye.

The conversation continued in a lively and fun-loving way. They got up and made their way to the bar, closer to the TVs. Grace and Cameron sat next to each other. Daniel took the seat next to Grace. That left Nick beside Cameron, on her other side.

After more talk about their jobs, the stormy, tropical Tampa weather, cool cars to buy some day, and clothing outlets, Nick leaned across the bar. "Hey, the ball game was so much fun," he said. "Sorry you weren't there, Grace. How about joining us for another game?"

"I don't know about baseball, but I like to talk and have a beer," Grace said and laughed. She had a big Southern smile and an accent that was fun to listen to.

"That's all it takes! You're in. I'll pick out a game or two and run it by Daniel and John. You know John, right?"

Grace responded, "Well, yes, I know Cameron, so I know John."

Eventually, both Daniel and Grace called it an evening. They had big days ahead. Nick and Cameron were alone. By 11:00 p.m. they had moved to a booth, where the conversation drifted back to Cameron's frustrations with her job. It turned out that Nick was a good listener, and because Cameron had had four glasses of wine and was talkative, there was plenty to listen to. Occasionally, he reached across the table and touched her hand. She could tell that he definitely had a sweet side, though she was still on guard.

Her phone rang, and she pushed it down deep into her purse. But it rang again, and reluctantly, she answered.

"I ran across a guy who I think was Jack Wilson," John said. "I was going to check on David Williams at the childcare facility. Sandra wasn't with me. This was earlier. And when I left, I saw Wilson riding a bike near the facility in the dark. We need to talk."

"So you went out again," Cameron said, trying not to let more disapproval creep into her voice.

"Don't start," John said.

She sighed. "I won't. But okay, let's talk."

"Are you at Sam's?"

"Yeah, but—"

"I'll be there in fifteen minutes."

Cameron sighed. "Shit," she said. It was terrible timing, but what could she do? "John's on his way. Something more to talk about with one of our cases. I'm sorry."

"It's okay," Nick said. "I get it. Listen, I was going to head out anyway." He stood up and reached out for a hug, and then he put his hands on her shoulders and kissed her on the lips. Cameron walked out the door with him and gave him a hug before saying goodbye.

Cameron went back into Sam's and sat alone, waiting for John. *That was nice*, she thought. Somehow, though, she wasn't as excited about it as she thought she might be. Nick was hot, and she loved that they seemed to be talking more, but she realized she wasn't taking her attraction to him very seriously.

After another ten minutes, John showed up. He looked worried. "Sorry to ruin your night, but my instincts are driving me crazy."

"What were you thinking?" she demanded, suddenly annoyed. She also realized that she was pretty tipsy, and it was getting late. She was tired.

"Sorry," John said again. "But I need to work with you on this. Jack Wilson hanging around close to Sandra's son is a problem."

"There's nothing we can do about it tonight," Cameron said.

John sighed. "Okay," he said. Then he looked at her. "You're drunk."

"Take me home, and you can pick me up in the morning. I'll just leave my car here. We can talk tomorrow. I'm not myself right now."

"No problem."

They left the bar and climbed into John's car, Cameron a bit unsteady. She dozed off on the drive. John pulled her out of the car and set her on her feet, and then he helped her along as she struggled to walk. By the time he stuffed her into the bed, it was midnight.

Chapter 40

UNDER THE BUS

John arrived at Cameron's apartment at 7:00 a.m. sharp the next morning, Wednesday. His banging on the door woke her up; she'd shut the alarm off when it went off an hour earlier. He hung out on the couch, sleepy himself, and listened to the shower, blow dryer, and toothbrush as Cameron threw herself together. She finally emerged from her bedroom forty-five minutes later, ready to go.

On the way to Sam's to pick up her car, Cameron struggled to stay awake as John talked. She offered a few comments about the upcoming hearing on the Halstrom matter, wondering how she was going to handle it. She'd drive straight to the courthouse to meet Lara Liu and Chad Burt. Maybe Chad could pull things together with Lara's help. They had the medical information from the hospital records and Dr. Camp's remarks. John was saying something about a visitation with David Williams, Sandra still at the Catholic charity home, Jack Wilson being near David's care facility, and something about Striker, who might be around too. Everything was foggy.

By the time John arrived at Sam's, Cameron was sound asleep. He turned around, pulled out of the parking lot, and headed to the courthouse. Cameron was still sleeping. She seemed to be vaguely with it by the time he pulled into the courthouse parking garage.

"What time is it?" Cameron asked.

"8:45."

"Good, we made it. Let's get up to the cattle call. Maybe it's a good thing you're here today as my backup."

Chad and Lara were already there, so Cameron and John huddled up with them in the crowded common assembly area. They managed to pull four chairs together to talk.

Cameron began. "Okay, the question is whether the state should continue to shelter Amy Jo. That's it, nothing else. This is not a hearing to determine whether the state is going to supervise Amy Jo and the Halstrom family long term, or whether the state wants to terminate the rights of the parents to be parents. We need to keep that in mind. This gives us somewhat of a shot to get Amy Jo released without further hearings and more work."

John looked at her in amusement. Hungover or not, she was managing to get it together professionally now.

Chad spoke up next. "Cameron, have you spoken to Stalnick about this?"

"No," she said. "And I don't really know how to handle him. He doesn't listen. I get that he's busy, but I'm busy too."

"I know," said Chad. "But is there a workaround here, some way to get him to accept your way of thinking? Maybe we should focus on that. Otherwise, he'll torpedo whatever you say as soon as the judge asks for your opinion. Even if he's your attorney, keep in mind that he can override you as the caseworker."

"Which is annoying," Cameron said.

Chad went on. "Now, Lara and I aren't bound by what Stalnick says. Lara is independent, and I represent her. Judge Crowe will open the hearing with a question to you, Cameron, so give her just the facts—no opinions—and your final conclusion, and then Lara and I can pick up the argument based on her conversation with the hospital doctor. Think about it: What can Stalnick do if he doesn't have evidence from you? Bottom line is the state attorney general's office is always just taking the most conservative position, trying to ensure they're not criticized. I'd be surprised if any judge thought otherwise."

"I'm no courtroom lawyer, but it makes sense to me," Lara said.

Chad looked at her. "Get ready; things do change," he said. "You'll have to tell the judge your findings."

A few minutes later, Stalnick entered the common area and spotted Cameron but said nothing. Instead, he struck up a conversation with a bailiff. That prompted Chad to inform the bailiff that the other interested parties were present and ready to address the court. Thirty minutes later, the bailiff summoned them. "All parties in Halstrom," he said. They filed into the courtroom, Stalnick first, without acknowledging or greeting the others. Obliged to follow protocol, Cameron sat directly beside him.

Judge Crowe appeared, and those in attendance introduced themselves. Mr. Halstrom and his sister showed up late. They gave their appearance, having gotten the hang of courtroom etiquette by now.

Judge Crowe nodded at Cameron. "Ms. Springer, anything new? Amy Jo Halstrom is still in custody. This is a continued shelter hearing."

"Yes, your honor, we continue to monitor this matter and to interview folks. On Monday, Dr. Camp interviewed Mary Halstrom and Charles Halstrom, separately, for a total of four hours. She told me that they present no danger to Amy Jo or her brothers. Mrs. Halstrom has agreed to some follow-up counseling. As noted before, she has emotional issues that need attention, nothing critical to the issues before the court. In addition, the guardian ad litem, Ms. Lara Liu, reviewed the hospital records and met with the attending physician who called the hotline."

Judge Crowe looked over at Lara. "Ms. Liu, do you have information helpful to these proceedings?"

"Yes, your honor. I reviewed the hospital records and spoke with the physician who attended to Amy Jo. The physician said there were no signs of child abuse. She detailed a hairline fracture of the upper arm bone, the humerus, and the fact that Amy Jo's shirt at the location of the upper right arm showed engrained soil and small rocks. This was suggestive of a fall. Your honor, as you know, I've been to the Halstrom house, and it's surrounded by grass, dirt, and gravel."

Judge Crowe asked, "So why was the child sheltered in the first place, and what is the evidence for continued shelter at this time, Ms. Springer?"

"Judge, I was told by deputy sheriffs at the house last week that the hospital had called the hotline with a charge of abuse. Maybe that was an error or maybe a failure in communication or simply not explained." Cameron was stone-faced, thinking, *Just the facts, just the facts.*

Judge Crowe set down her pencil, looking like she didn't know what to say. Then she picked it up again, made a note, and turned to Mr. Stalnick.

"Mr. Stalnick. Under the circumstances, what is the position of the state?"

Stalnick rose. "This is all news to me. I've heard nothing of this."

"Well," the judge said, "you've heard it now. What did Ms. Springer tell you before the hearing?"

"Judge, I was tied up dealing with another case. I didn't speak with her."

Judge Crowe said nothing, and silence infused the courtroom as she sat back and made some more notes. "I'm going back to chambers, Mr. Stalnick. Please speak with Ms. Springer and determine the position of the state. I will be back in a few minutes."

"Yes, your honor."

The judge left.

Stalnick turned to Cameron and said, "Let's step outside."

Once outside, Stalnick laid into her. "You threw me under the bus! Do it again and this will be your last case. Do you understand?" He looked furious and didn't bother to keep his voice down.

John came up to them, having heard the attorney's words.

When John showed up, Cameron took a step back.

John said, "Stalnick, you're out of line. This caseworker has been working hard dealing with three difficult cases, and you've volunteered no help at all."

Cameron became wide-eyed. She put her hands on her hips and glared at Stalnick.

John continued. "And you could have consulted with her before the hearing when we were all sitting in the same room. She didn't throw you under the bus; you crawled there. Now, figure out the state's position as an attorney and get on with it."

"Thanks for the help, Quint; you're just as useless." Stalnick stormed back into the courtroom.

Cameron dropped her hands by her side and looked up at John. She said quietly, "Thank you," and reached out to touch his hand. With that, she walked back to the courtroom.

John followed. After they took their seats, it was another five minutes of awkward silence before Judge Crowe appeared.

"Mr. Stalnick, as the attorney for the state of Florida, what's the state's position?"

"No position, your honor."

"Well, based on the information reported today, the court finds that it is duty bound to release Amy Jo from shelter. The state has made no arguments and stated no reason to justify keeping Amy Jo from the custody of her parents. Further, the court notes that the state filed no dependency petition for the court to exercise protective supervision over Amy Jo. Therefore, in all respects, the state shall release Amy Jo to her parents and at this point exercise no continued protective supervision. This hearing is over. You're all excused."

Everyone filed back out, and Stalnick, passing by Cameron, said, "I'm the attorney, not you. I represent the state. You work for the state and for me. You better hope those Halstrom kids are safe, because it's your neck on the line." Cameron just looked at him, saying nothing. Then Chad spoke up.

"Cameron, I'm proud of you, and, Lara, you too. Stalnick deserved a back seat on this one."

John rushed ahead and stepped in front of the state's attorney. Stalnick brushed him aside, but John lectured him as he kept walking. "You've got this backward," John said. "We work for the state, and you're supposed to be our counsel. Instead, you stick your head in the sand and don't listen to the facts. What are you afraid of? Is it Cameron? You should be. She's tough and smart."

The others caught up with them, and Chad grabbed John by the arm. "Let it go, John. We get it. We can expect some repercussions on account of this—disciplinary stuff. Let me know. I'll vouch for you guys."

"Me too," Lara added. "I know this was serious, but it was hilarious, too. I didn't realize it would be so entertaining. Anyway, I'm happy for the Halstrom family, and I sure hope they keep it together."

Cameron walked along with her head down, lips pursed, wiping her eyes as she fought back tears. "The Halstroms will. That's the least of our worries."

They headed back to their respective offices. Cameron thanked John for sticking up for her. "Are we going to lose our jobs over this?" she asked.

John shrugged. "Don't worry about that," he said. "I just couldn't stand that guy laying into you like that. He's an asshole; you're right."

Waves of exhaustion rose in Cameron again, and she said, "I'm toast. I'm so tired right now, and I have to go visit with Alisha, do some follow-up there. She's probably home with Elijah. I wonder if Juan Martinez is taking care of the kid today. Do you mind if I nap again while you drive me to get my car?"

John shook his head. "No problem," he said.

Chapter 41

RIDDLES AND MYSTERIES

John left Cameron with her car and headed back to the office, thinking that maybe he ought to give his superiors a rundown on the morning's events. Cameron went straight to her apartment to rest before jumping back into the fray. Hopefully, she'd have an informative and helpful discussion with Alisha. And it had been quite a morning, with Stalnick threatening her the way he had. The judge had just asked for the facts, and she and Lara had provided exactly that. At least the morning had a good outcome, with Amy Jo being released.

Did anyone really appreciate their work? Cameron wondered about that. It was so rare to receive even a simple "thank you" or "good job." Maybe it was time for her to think about doing something else. Could Grace help her, maybe give her some suggestions? Of course, John was always a help, and then last night with Nick, there had been a connection there too. *At least I have options*, she told herself.

Two hours later, she headed over to the West Tampa Café. There were some local politicians there, but no one else Cameron knew, no friends. She sat at a table alone, trying to energize herself. She decided she was tired of not understanding all the conversation going on around her and resolved to learn some Spanish.

After a quick lunch, she drove over to Alisha's. She wasn't home, but Juan Martinez answered the door and invited Cameron in for another look around. Elijah was napping. Cameron checked on him, and he was fine.

"I'm back babysitting today," Juan said. "Alisha called me this morning and said she had another job tip. She's working at it, that's for sure. I can tell by how much pay I've lost over the last month. No problem. I like the little guy. He's better than a dog. Just kidding. I change him, but I don't have to walk him. It's hot enough outside at the docks."

Cameron was back to listening carefully to every word, alert to potential animosity or belligerence, making sure he was in a friendly mood. She concluded that he sounded okay. "I appreciate your speaking with me and being friendly again—I'm actually kind of surprised. I thought you didn't like me, and maybe you still don't. Unfortunately, we've just run into a lot of not-good experiences with the boyfriends who date single moms in the cases we work on. So that's why I need to check in. Can you understand that?"

He nodded. "I get it. Nothing's perfect. I'm not really a boyfriend though. Or at least not right now."

"Okay," Cameron said, waiting to see if he'd volunteer anything else.

"Anyway, isn't it Elijah you're really here for?"

"For Elijah and Alisha both. You know Alisha's history, I assume."

"Sure," he said. "Give me your version."

"Nope." She tilted her head and raised her eyebrows. "That's Alisha's job, not mine."

"No problem. I know enough. Believe me."

"I get it. To me, she seems to keep to herself," Cameron remarked.

"Not to me," Juan said, shrugging.

"What's that mean?"

"What you see is what you get. There's no mystery."

"Okay, but that seems like a riddle to me."

"Riddle—no, no riddle. With her, it's always in front of you."

"Juan, I don't get it. What's in front of me?"

"I don't mean no disrespect, but you don't see it, do you?"

Cameron was frustrated; Juan seemed to be riddling her himself. "What's going on? Why don't you just tell me?"

"Sorry, Ms. Cameron Springer. Believe it or not, I basically like you. No disrespect. I know you had to talk about me in court—Alisha told me—and I gave you a hard time last week."

"Okay, Juan, thank you. But I need to know the bottom line. If there's a problem with Alisha, I need to know."

"Look," he said, "I'm her friend, and I like her, but I'm not sold on getting totally wrapped up with her. I'm going to say this, but don't repeat it."

Cameron shook her head. "Don't ask me to not repeat what you tell me. It's my job to do that with any information I can learn."

Juan instantly stopped talking and just sat there. She stared at him, and he stared back and then tilted his head and gazed into space. That went on for about a minute. Looking back at her, he raised both hands up, shook his head, and said, "No. I'm not going to talk to you anymore, not today, anyway."

"Okay, Juan, but what about Elijah? Is he safe?"

He said nothing.

Now Cameron was on alert. "So he's not safe."

"I didn't say that." He pointed a finger at her sternly.

"I need to know what you mean."

Juan said nothing. "Fine," Cameron said. She got up and went to the door and opened it, as if to leave.

"Wait," Juan said.

"Okay. So tell me something then."

He shook his head again. "Look, if I say this to you, I might lose Alisha."

"How?"

"By talking to you."

"Sorry." Cameron sat back down, waiting.

"Okay. So you know Alisha has lots of friends, people in the neighborhood. All kinds of people. It's easy for her. Yeah, she can be closed but only when she's afraid or thinks she needs to be into just herself. So the two friends I saw late last night, when I was just leaving . . . I didn't say anything about it to Alisha. She knows them too, couldn't be nicer to them. I was looking out the window and saw them outside."

"When was this?" Cameron asked.

"Last night."

"Okay. Go on."

"The first one saw me and left, I'm pretty sure. The other showed up a few minutes later. He looked weird, moving around kind of slow, like he's trying not to be seen. I couldn't tell what was going on, but one or both of them looked like they were up to something. I stuck around until they left a few minutes later."

"Do you know their names?" Cameron said.

"The first was Wilson, Josh Wilson. The other one's called Striker or something."

Cameron took a breath. "Does Josh have big tattoos on his arms?"

"Yeah," Juan replied.

"Blue arrows, purple flowers?"

"Sounds about right. It was dark, but I've seen those tattoos before."

"His name was Josh?" Cameron asked.

"Yeah, that's his name, Josh."

"Or maybe Jack?"

"Yeah, that's it. Jack."

"Okay, Juan. When Alisha gets back, she needs to call me right away. That guy is bad news. We don't know for sure, but we've been on the lookout for him. Can you stay here?"

Juan nodded. "Yeah, I can stay. But what's up here? You're not going to tell me?"

Cameron shook her head. "I can't," she said. "Please trust me, just this once. At this point, you're all I've got."

He looked at her and then nodded, seeming to accept this.

"Call the police if they show back up," Cameron said. She hustled out the door, leaving a worried-looking Juan to stay behind.

Chapter 42

A FEW MINUTES

Cameron arrived back at the office, hot and sweaty and still intense. "We have a problem," she said to John when she reached his cubicle.

"Oh?" He was all ears.

"Late last night, Jack Wilson and your friend Striker showed up at Alisha's. Juan Martinez said it seemed like they were up to something."

John frowned. "Oh, that's bad. At a minimum, a serious risk. What sort of connection could there be? It's very strange."

"No shit. Juan told me they were friends of Alisha. Those guys sure get around."

"I think we need to get Alisha and Elijah out of there, to a safe house like the place for Sandra. I can't bear the thought of something happening like it did to Sandra."

Cameron nodded. "Right. We don't know for sure, but the police have been wondering about those two guys for a week, just like we have. What makes you think Alisha will go?"

"I don't know," John said. "But I doubt they just showed up out of thin air. But if we get Alisha's consent, we can always get her into one of our residential facilities for just one night. We can come up with something longer term later. If she doesn't cooperate, we're going to need some type of court order. I doubt we can convince the police to stake out the apartment overnight on a hunch, and even if we could, that would only be a short-term solution. But we still have no solid evidence of real risk. I'm just not sure how far we'll get with the police or the judge. But we absolutely cannot deal with this by ourselves. Even I get that now."

"I wonder if Alisha's mother can help," Cameron mused.

"That's something to think about," John said. "Maybe she could take Elijah overnight."

"I can't file court papers on my own," Cameron said. "Stalnick is the attorney assigned to them. I'm going to have to go see him. This sucks."

"I know, but I don't see another option."

"Look, John, can you run over to Alisha's, see if you can find her and get her to cooperate? And maybe just do quick checks on Sandra and David Williams."

John nodded. "That works. I'll see you later. If you hear from Alisha, call me, and vice versa." He left.

Cameron called the deputy attorney general's office. "This is Stalnick," he said brusquely when he picked up the line.

"This is Cameron Springer. I'm sorry to bother you, but I need to meet with you this afternoon. I think I have an emergency, and I need your assistance. This is critical, in my opinion." She decided to just get to the point.

"What's this about?"

"Last week Sandra Williams was beaten. Fortunately, her child, David, was in shelter at the time. There's more than a reasonable possibility the beating was done by one or two young men we've identified. They've now been spotted at the apartment of Alisha Santeroa, who has custody of her young son, Elijah. And one was recently spotted hanging around the shelter where David Williams is staying. We think we need to move Alisha and Elijah, but we're not sure she'll cooperate. I had a worrisome experience with her in court last week. She doesn't trust me."

"No surprise," Stalnick said.

"Okay," Cameron said. "Look, I know how you feel about me. Now this is beyond just me. Sandra was in the hospital for days, almost in a coma from the beating. This goes well beyond what you think about me. You're the attorney on the case, and you missed a hearing last week. This isn't easy for me, but you understand what I'm saying."

After a brief pause, Stalnick relented. "I have a few minutes free later this afternoon," he said. "Maybe I'll ask an associate lawyer to join us for observation."

"I can accept that. I'll be down in thirty minutes. Thank you." Cameron hung up the phone and left for downtown, thinking that it hadn't been so bad.

When John got to Alisha's apartment, Juan Martinez was still there, playing with Elijah. Nothing seemed amiss.

"Well, two in one day," Juan said. "Alisha's still not here."

At Juan's invitation, John walked in and glanced around. "Hi there," he said to Elijah.

"Have a seat," Juan said. "Everything is A-okay here."

"Have you heard from Alisha?"

"No."

"Can you call her?"

"She don't have any money for a cell phone."

John nodded. It was obvious that there was not a lot of money to be had. "When did she say she'd be home?"

"She didn't say. She's on the bus system, so there's no telling."

"Mind if I wait? I'll just . . . I don't know, read this motorcycle magazine," he said, grabbing the first one on the coffee table.

Juan shrugged amiably. "Hang around here as long as you want. But I've got to get back to my place no later than 10:00. Can't miss another day of work."

John remembered to call the two beat cops he knew to ask about surveillance, and they told him they'd try but couldn't guarantee it. At least it was something.

Chapter 43

OUTSIDE THE BOX

Cameron got to Stalnick's office and signed in with the receptionist, who was also some type of security guard. Admission to the attorney general's office in Tampa required a code, pass, or permission from the receptionist, even if it was just a bunch of local deputy attorneys working there. The waiting area offered one chair and one picture. The ragged chair had clearly been in use for years. The picture was of some state politician, maybe an attorney general. The floor was carpeted instead of the usual governmental linoleum. Naturally, Cameron had to wait.

Stalnick came out in about fifteen minutes. His office suggested someone with taste, and there was a photograph of an attractive family with young children. Cameron gave him the same information about Wilson and Striker in greater detail. He and the other deputy attorney he'd asked to sit in—a friendly woman, dressed very professionally—both listened to the details in silence.

Then she decided to address what had happened earlier in Judge Crowe's courtroom to clear the air, if possible.

"I didn't intend to usurp your responsibilities or authority," Cameron started out. "The judge asked me about the current status and the information obtained over the last two days. Lara and I gave the report, factually and without embellishment or drama. I didn't make any recommendations. Then the judge asked you about the state's position. Anyway, because we had not spoken beforehand, we were both put in a difficult position."

"Springer, that's basically correct, but you have a misapprehension of my position. I'm a deputy attorney general and, in that sense, I'm an extension of the attorney general of the state of Florida, an official of the state elected by the people and exercising all powers of that office. I'm not just a regular attorney. Therefore, you don't make policy or substantive decisions as to the state's position before the court. I do, on behalf of the state, and you have no authority to decide the position of the state without my approval. You overstepped. You should have briefed me beforehand. Instead, you sat on your hands even though I was in the common area and freely available to you and your little cabal."

"Okay, I accept that. As a practical matter, I do make decisions every day about these kids and their families. That's the way it is. I work hard, try to do my best, and, you know, I'm bound to make mistakes. It's impossible not to. I agree I should have discussed this with you in the common area. I hope you understand the circumstances. Anyway, here I am. Can we lay this morning aside and deal with this new situation?"

Stalnick wasn't stupid, Cameron realized—just arrogant. If he shuffled her off and something bad happened, his neck would be on the line. She didn't care about control at this point; she just needed his help.

After a minute, he said, "It might be a problem getting the sheriff to unilaterally pick up Elijah again and place him in overnight shelter. And Alisha, as an adult, is too old to put in shelter. She remains in the state's system only under the independent living program for those who have aged out of the system. But the state can't exercise control over her, so the matter falls into a gray zone. But I don't think there's any harm in asking for direction from the court."

"Do you think we could get a court order to have the sheriff pick up both Alisha and Elijah?" Cameron asked hopefully.

Stalnick thought for a minute and then said he would file an emergency motion and see what happened. Judge Crowe's judicial assistant called to say that the court would hold a hearing at 5:30 p.m. that day and to request that Stalnick make sure Alisha knew of the hearing time.

"Thank you," Cameron said.

"You're welcome," said Stalnick. "And you're right to call me on this. We're glad to pitch in. Let's see what happens."

Cameron called John, who was still at Alisha's apartment. He agreed to transport Alisha to the courthouse if and when she arrived, but there was no way he could guarantee what would happen.

Cameron, Stalnick, and his associate attorney showed up before Judge Crowe at 5:30 p.m. The common assembly area was full, and all of the five judges assigned to child welfare were still conducting hearings.

"So," Judge Crowe said, addressing both Stalnick and Cameron, "are matters worse or better? While the court appreciates brevity, this notice claims an emergency because of an imminent risk of physical violence but gives no particulars—no names, no specific circumstances, no details of the risk. I suppose there's a reason? Give me the details, Mr. Stalnick?"

"Judge," Stalnick began, "I'll need to turn this over to Ms. Springer on the factual details. I think your honor will see that there are some legal hurdles to discuss. I'm ready to review with the court as your honor requests. I should say this is an unusual request: a request for authorization to bring Elijah Santeroa into shelter this evening and, with the cooperation of Alisha Santeroa, authority to house her overnight as well."

"Do we have her cooperation? If so, you don't need the court's assistance."

"That makes sense, Judge, but we think an order from you may persuade Ms. Santeroa to go along with this shelter plan. The sheriff can always take and shelter Elijah upon your order, followed by a shelter hearing tomorrow morning, but Ms. Santeroa—although within the independent living program of the state—is an adult. She's not open to arrest, which is what taking her into custody would amount to. She has done nothing wrong, to the state's knowledge."

Judge Crowe noted that she had removed Elijah from shelter the previous week after a fully argued hearing with all present. "Is the situation different now?" She turned to Cameron.

Cameron looked at Stalnick, not about to step on his toes again. He waved his arm, inviting her to proceed.

"We hope there's no risk," she said. "However, we also hope we can locate Alisha and persuade her to go with her son into a protected shelter, at least for the evening. Barring that, we hope the sheriff would heed an order of this court permitting shelter of Elijah again. We already have police surveillance of their apartment, but they can't guarantee it round the clock."

"Anything else?" the judge probed.

"My superior, John Quint, is at the apartment right now. We had hoped Ms. Santeroa would have arrived before this hearing, so he could provide notice and bring them here. However, it's now apparent that did not happen, and he has to leave soon to check on two other clients, Sandra Williams and her son, David. They seem to be at risk as well, but they are both in some form of shelter already."

Judge Crowe looked at Cameron intently. "How are Sandra and David Williams at risk, and how is that relevant in this case?"

Cameron continued. "Sandra was severely beaten in her apartment last week, but she remembers nothing. She was released from the hospital, and we then secured protective shelter for her. David was already in shelter, per your honor's order. However, as we monitored the situation, we received information that two persons suspected of involvement in the beating of Sandra were seen near the place of protective custody for David and also at Alisha Santeroa's apartment. The police have identified these two individuals as persons of interest in the beating of Sandra Williams. And now, this week, someone unknown, maybe one of the two, broke into Ms. Williams's and trashed the place. Based on information learned this afternoon, we know the two were at Alisha's apartment last night. Where they are now, we do not know."

"You or Mr. Quint saw the two suspects at Ms. Santeroa's apartment?"

"No, your honor, Mr. Quint observed one of them last night near the shelter of David, which is highly suspicious. How could Jack Wilson know about the location of the shelter? I also conducted an interview with Juan Martinez this afternoon."

Judge Crowe pressed for clarification. "Mr. Martinez? Isn't that the paramour you complained about last week?"

"Yes, he is, your honor. But since then, we've met with him and followed up with his labor union and have gained trust in him. He told me the two suspects were at Ms. Santeroa's apartment last night as he was leaving. This seems highly coincidental."

"What can this court do at this time? This seems to be a matter for the sheriff and the police," Judge Crowe said.

"Judge," Stalnick spoke up, "stranger things can happen, but in this circumstance, the state asks the court to address this somewhat outside the box. Shelter is usually addressed to the court after a minor is already placed in shelter. And shelter for an adult is not within the court's power—we understand that. Given the ruling last week taking Elijah out of shelter, asking the sheriff to bring him back into shelter may be the only way to get some action. Our thought is that the court's order would clarify the matter as to Elijah. And, while the court cannot order Alisha into shelter, there's nothing to prevent the court suggesting that Alisha agree to shelter at least for tonight, and then maybe by tomorrow we can get a better handle on this. Ms. Santeroa appeared respectful of the court last week. It may carry over if we can find her."

Judge Crowe nodded, ready to issue her decision. "Taking into account the entirety of the circumstances, the court finds it has jurisdiction in the case of Elijah Santeroa to find probable cause for the sheriff to take him into shelter, followed by a hearing tomorrow at 10:00 a.m. The court also suggests that his mother, Alisha Santeroa, voluntarily accept protective shelter from the state. If she accepts, she is free to come and go as she pleases. The court further suggests the shelter for the mother and son to be the same. So ordered. Mr. Stalnick, please type up this order. I will sign it before we recess this evening. Can you get it to me in a few minutes, by 7:00?"

"Yes, your honor." With that, Stalnick walked out of the courtroom with Cameron in tow. "Good work," he said to her. "Glad I was able to help. Hang around with me until I get a copy of the signed order. You may get an opportunity to show it to Alisha tonight and to the sheriff."

Cameron felt on edge, her mind racing. Judge Crowe was totally on top of things, completely in line with Cameron's presentation and concerns, and ready to act without hesitation. And somehow Stalnick had now come around to her way of thinking as well. All in all, the afternoon had gone well.

Chapter 44

COURT ORDER

John kept hoping Alisha would show up, but eventually he had to head off to see Sandra and David.

When he left, Juan was feeding Elijah cooked beans, pasta with tomato sauce, cut-up bananas, and Cheerios. Elijah was in a chair and eating with his fingers, obviously hungry. Juan seemed to be exactly the opposite of what Cameron had thought of him last week; now, it was clear that he was a caring and supportive friend.

John got to the Catholic charity residential unit in twenty minutes. In midsummer Tampa, it was still light, though dusk was coming. The sun was dropping nearer to the horizon. It would be dark by 8:30.

Sandra was not there. He asked an attendant where she was. Had she gone for a walk? No, the attendant didn't think so. Did she have a ride? Again, the attendant didn't know. He thought Sandra was just leaving for a few minutes.

"Did she say anything about David?" John asked.

The attendant thought about it. He said, "Give me a minute or two. You certainly ask a lot of questions."

John said, "Yeah, sorry about that. I'm with Kids Care."

"That's good. I remember now. The answer is yes. She seemed happy, said she'd be spending some time with him."

John called Cameron to fill her in. "I don't know if everyone's okay, but I hope so," he said. "Sandra isn't here at the residence. The attendant says she went to see David, but I'm not sure how she would do that. All was good at Alisha's apartment when I left there. Juan was feeding Elijah. Alisha never showed."

Cameron didn't know what to say. She gave John a rundown on the hearing before Judge Crowe.

"Believe it or not, Stalnick supported me," Cameron said. "He's definitely arrogant, but I guess that's the way the guy's wired. Oh, here he is now with the order—hold on."

John heard Stalnick saying, "Here's a copy of the order signed by the judge. I'll try to get someone at the sheriff's child investigation unit to respond this evening, but I don't have too much hope in that. In the meantime, can you get it to Alisha?"

"I'll try," Cameron said. "Thanks for the help."

"Well, I think we've done what we can. We'll see what happens. I'll call you if I get the order to a deputy sheriff and action is taken. If I don't call, that means I got no assistance, at least this evening."

"Okay, thanks," Cameron said. "I'm on the phone with John, so I'll leave now. Good night." After a few seconds, she said to John, "Did you catch that? I'm out of his office now."

"Yes, good. And you got an order. That's a miracle. I guess you and Stalnick kissed and made up."

"Ha ha," Cameron said. "Kind of. Anyway, he came through for us this evening. The judge was super helpful too. Anyway, we still have work to do tonight. I'll head over to Alisha's and wait it out."

"Okay," John said. "I may just troll around here in my car for a bit, see if Sandra shows up, and then one way or another I'll shoot over to check on David. That's the plan, and I think I should stick to it. You might see some police at Alisha's, so if you do, check in with them. Juan's taking care of Elijah."

"Sounds good," Cameron said. "Keep me posted."

After hanging up, John drove around block after block near the Catholic facility and never saw Sandra or anything to suggest she was still around. Not sure what to make of this, he changed strategies and drove to the shelter where David was lodged.

Chapter 45

DUMPED

When John arrived at David's residential facility, it was almost totally dark. The parking lot was mostly empty, except for the cars belonging to employees. The facility was in north Tampa, a quasi-urban area with a lot of people but spread out among woodlands and cypress swamps. There were alligators in ditches, small lakes, creeks, and the river nearby. Native Floridians knew to take care and leash their pets.

The parked cars were empty save one with a woman sitting in the driver's seat, windows rolled down, smoking a cigarette. John walked toward the facility, glancing at the occupied car. Something didn't seem right. He felt a little more comfortable once he reached the door and buzzed to enter. A woman looked at him through a window and asked his name. He handed her an identification badge through a slot, and she admitted him into an unoccupied reception area. She confirmed that Sandra was there, in a room set up for supervised visitation between parents and sheltered children.

John was relieved when he found her. "Hi," he said. "I see you and David are enjoying some free time."

"How'd you find me?" Sandra asked, looking surprised. She looked up at John. She was sitting next to David on the floor, playing with blocks.

"I didn't. I came to check on David. I looked for you at the Catholic residence."

"What's up?"

"No big cause for alarm, but we spotted Jack Wilson and maybe Striker hanging around here, and also over at Alisha Santeroa's apartment. Do you know Alisha?"

"Yeah, but I don't see her too often. She's around. She knows everybody, including Jack and Striker. They're friends."

"You know we're concerned about them," John said, sitting down next to Sandra and David. He started to play with the blocks too.

"Hello, build castle right here," David said, pointing to some other blocks.

Sandra joined the building effort and then stopped and looked over at John. She suddenly looked nervous. "Yeah, me too; I'm concerned," she said.

"Why?" John asked. He hoped she'd say more.

After a minute of tense silence, Sandra said, "I'm scared to death. It's probably Jack who beat me, but I don't really know. I dumped him, but I tried to be honest about it. I said it was over. I don't know. Sometimes he doesn't take things too good. But Striker's harmless. He's always helping people. He leads a strange life. He's got some money, but he never has a place to stay. He's out on the streets, with friends—that sort of stuff. Not many people like that."

"Okay," John said. "Can you tell me any more?"

"Jack, that guy's a mistake. I know why I did that. I just latch on. I see that. He'd hurt me sometimes. I promised myself not again with that. I beat the drugs. I think the new place will help. They're nice. I'm getting better. Please don't take David away. Is that why you're here?"

"No, don't worry about that. I'm here for you and David. So is Cameron. The two of you are under our watch. We want you to get settled and get David back. Do you understand?"

"God, I hope so. He's the only thing I got now. He's my hope."

"Who's the woman in the car?" John said, figuring he'd give it a shot.

"She's a friend. Met her yesterday. She gave me a ride."

John frowned. "Sandra, is she safe?"

"I think so," Sandra said.

"Where'd you meet her?"

"At a restaurant on the corner just down from the new apartment. We got to talking about David, and she felt sorry for me."

"What's she do?" This was sounding suspicious to John, but he didn't want to alarm Sandra any more than necessary.

"I don't know," Sandra said, shaking her head. "She lives in one of the apartments around the corner. She's a lot older than me. It's not a drug thing, if you're worried about that. I swear."

"No," said John. "I believe you." He did, but all his instincts also told him that something was off about this.

Sandra stood up and handed David to the attendant. He started to cry.

"My heart is breaking," Sandra said.

"I understand," John said. "We'll work together; we'll get there. Here, I'll walk you to the car."

Chapter 46

SWAMP WATCH

During the time John was out looking for Sandra, Striker was on his own mission, another walk about town. He asked himself what he was doing; he could be crashing at the drug house or somewhere else—not Alisha's, of course, and not Sandra's, for that matter, given her mystery absence. But he couldn't answer the question. Deep inside, he knew there was a reason, but he didn't know what it was. He just had to be out and about, impelled by some unrecognized force.

He glanced over at a swampy area adjacent to a parking lot. He was sure he saw a flash of white, just a quick moment of light. The swamp was dark, with tall cypress trees laden with hanging moss, but a light from a building about fifty yards away streamed across the lot and faded away across it. There was a thin growth of ferns and water-based plants. Striker walked along the sidewalk in the shadows of trees and bushes, but once he saw the flash of white light, he slid into the dark. He settled into a squat, keeping himself out of view. His shirt was black, so he figured he couldn't be easily spotted. He kept staring at the place where the flash had briefly appeared. This time, he saw it move. It was a person for sure. Confirming his intuition, a man with a white face appeared and then ducked back into the murky swamp. It was Jack Wilson. Striker knew it was him—there was no mistaking that white, white face. What was he doing? It looked like he was surveying the parking lot adjacent to the swamp, and maybe the building, too.

Of course, Striker thought: that was the reason for his walkabout. He'd tracked Wilson the night before, too, around Alisha's apartment. Something was going on, and Striker didn't feel good about it, especially given the things Wilson had said about Sandra and weird ramblings about his messed-up childhood and mother. It all felt off.

Striker began to move, slowly and carefully, sometimes crawling along the ground, working his way across from the other side of the swamp. From there, he figured he could surveil from a point behind Wilson, assuming the man's attention was focused ahead on the parking lot and the building. He got as close as he could and then he settled down to watch. Every so often, he could see Wilson's shadow move.

He looked carefully for any glaring eyes of alligators in the swamp or on its banks, but all he saw were the eyes of raccoons or opossums. The moon wasn't full, but it did cast some light on the scene. But for Wilson's movements, everything was still. There wasn't even a breeze. Wilson seemed to be stalking something, just as he had the night before, at Alisha's. Why had Wilson gone there? Was he the one with the mask who had trashed Sandra's? Wilson wasn't wearing a mask now, so maybe not.

At the same time, Striker saw Sandra and John leave the building. They were talking and making their way toward the already occupied car. Striker rubbed his eyes and did a double take: yes, it was Sandra, and she was with the guy who had been stalking Striker before. What was he doing with her? Was this good or bad? Striker couldn't tell.

Then Wilson charged out of the swamp, something big in his right hand. It was a piece of lumber, a two-by-four.

When he was just about to the car, John looked back over his left shoulder. Sandra was on his right. Wilson struck John on the back of the head with the two-by-four and knocked him to the pavement. Sandra screamed, "Stop! Stop it, Jack!"

The woman in the car started the engine and sped off. Sandra was screaming, and beating on Wilson's back as he kicked John. Sandra turned to run, but Wilson grabbed her with his left arm, dropped the wood, and swung his right fist into her face. When she fell, he kicked her until she lost consciousness. John struggled to get up. He got up, but Wilson knocked him down and hit him again, this time with his fist. John stopped moving. Wilson kicked him again.

Striker charged. He tackled Wilson and they both hit the pavement hard. Wilson picked up the wood and hit Striker across his back. Striker struggled to his feet as Wilson tore off in the direction of the swamp. In a few minutes, Striker heard sirens.

Striker struggled to regain his footing. Wilson was gone. Striker could think and he could move, but when he tried to straighten up, he moaned with pain. He ran across the street, bent over, avoiding the swamp and heading into the surrounding neighborhood, which was dark and woodsy, an old neighborhood with plenty of trees and cover. He edged back toward the swamp, hoping to tail Wilson and keep himself in the shadows. It looked like Wilson was headed in the direction of Alisha's apartment, which was not far away.

As best he could, Striker moved quickly through backyards, traversing ditches, hurdling or climbing fences. He tried to keep quiet, but his movements attracted the neighborhood dogs, who started barking and howling.

Striker was sure Wilson hadn't spotted him crossing the street. He was sure that Wilson had recognized him when he hit him, but maybe he didn't know that Striker was following him. Glancing through a backyard, Striker caught a glimpse of Wilson's flashing white face as he ran out onto the sidewalk on the next street and turned right. Yes! His gut was right: Wilson was going to Alisha's. Striker was charged up with adrenaline now, no longer feeling any pain.

He had to get to Alisha's before Wilson did.

Chapter 47

DEAD WRONG

After she received the court's order from Stalnick, Cameron drove to Alisha's apartment. She tried calling John, but there was no answer. It was getting late. She knocked on Alisha's door. Juan answered and invited her in.

The cops were outside, but Cameron knew they had to leave occasionally to answer other calls, other problems. Juan told her that he'd decided to hang around. Elijah was asleep when Cameron arrived.

She wondered about John. Where was he? He'd gone to check on David, but why hadn't she heard anything? And what about Jack Wilson and Striker—where were those guys now? Keeping her thoughts to herself, she watched television with Juan.

Cameron and Juan heard voices outside around 11:30. It was Alisha. They went to the window to peer out.

"Ma'am, please stop," one of the cops was saying to Alisha. "Everything is all right, but we need to check with you."

"What for?"

"We have this apartment complex under surveillance for the evening. Can you give us some identification and what apartment you're headed to?"

"I don't have a driver's license, but I have a card with my name and address on it from DCF," Alisha said. "I live in that apartment, number three on the second floor, with the lights on."

"Thank you. Let's walk up to the apartment together, if you don't mind."

"Is Elijah all right? Is that why you're here?"

"Yes, ma'am, Elijah is inside asleep. Let's go upstairs." Cameron and Juan looked at each other and waited by the door.

When she opened the door, Alisha saw Cameron, and her features darkened. "What are you doing here? You scared me to death. Where's Elijah?" She shot a dirty look in Juan's direction. "Why'd you let her in?"

"Alisha, calm down and I'll explain," Cameron said. She nodded to the beat cops, who started walking away toward the stairs. Cameron stepped back and motioned to a couch. "Let's sit down for a second."

Alisha didn't move, so Cameron sat down. She realized she was in a vulnerable position and said again to Alisha, "Let's talk."

Juan kept standing. Alisha just stared at Cameron, hands on her hips, but after a few seconds she sat down, saying, "I'm sitting only to hear you out, but this is unreal. What reason could you have for being here this late?"

"We've been monitoring this neighborhood the last few days," Cameron explained. "One of our clients was severely beaten a few days ago and ended up in the hospital. Two men who were here last night were also seen near the sheltered residence of the child of the woman who was assaulted: Jack Wilson and Striker. You know them, right?"

Alisha squinted at Cameron. "So? I haven't done anything. You'd better not have said anything, Juan." Juan remained standing, speechless.

Cameron looked hard at Alisha and then said, "Look. You're not being honest with me. If you were, we might not be here. But these two friends or whatever are very dangerous, at least by all appearances."

Alisha stood up and leaned over to Cameron, face to face, only a few inches apart. "You're dead wrong, as always. Now get out!"

"I have a court order," Cameron said.

Suddenly, there was a crash from Elijah's bedroom. Jack Wilson burst into the front room, swinging his fists and kicking. Everything happened fast. Wilson knocked Juan down, striking his head with a lead pipe. He threw Alisha against the wall. Cameron grabbed Jack's leg, but he smashed her arms with the pipe.

The police barged in. *Thank God*, Cameron thought. She was on the floor, dazed. Her arms throbbed with pain. One of the officers went over to Alisha, who was slumped against the wall. The other quickly checked Juan, who pulled himself upright, clearly badly hurt.

"Elijah," he said, gesturing toward the bedroom. The officer raced to the room.

Cameron and Juan looked at each other. "I'm all right," she said, even though she wasn't. "But—"

The officer came back into the room and said, "There's no one in there." Cameron gasped. That meant that Wilson had taken Elijah and escaped.

Chapter 48

TRACKED

Striker was about thirty yards from the back of the apartment complex when he heard a crash. He had just nestled on all fours behind a bush and two garbage cans. His head jerked up, and he looked over the cans toward the sound. *Wilson.* He was on the ground where he'd fallen, and the second-floor window above Wilson was open. A ladder was on the ground. Striker saw Wilson get up and grapple with a large bundle. Striker looked harder. It was a kid. Wilson had Elijah!

Striker saw Wilson hoist up the kid and run to the opposite yard. *Damn,* Striker thought. He was still hunched over and grimaced with each movement, but he had to get moving.

As a night owl, Striker was familiar with the territory. But hours after midnight, he still hadn't even glimpsed Wilson. Somehow, Wilson had managed to slip away with Elijah, and Striker had no idea where he might take him. He worried that the boy was already dead. Surely, the kid should be crying, but he heard nothing. Maybe Wilson had gagged him, or the kid was knocked out.

Striker hobbled through the neighborhood on high alert. Although he had no actual, hardcore fear of the police, he preferred to avoid them. And he knew he had a better chance of finding Elijah if he was alone. He knew Wilson, and he knew how to scavenge through the neighborhood.

At an old house, he wedged himself into the crawl space underneath, waiting and watching for a break. The police were everywhere, though there were no dogs—not yet. Then Striker found himself hoping that the police would find Wilson and Elijah before he did. He was hurt, and Wilson had already beat him up once. He found himself having a bit of hope in the police, which wasn't natural.

It was close to daybreak and still dark when Striker got a break. There was no full moon. It was quiet. The police must have ventured off to another part of the neighborhood. Suddenly, Striker spotted Wilson. There was his white face, ducking and crawling around under houses across the street. Striker didn't see Elijah.

He saw Wilson again—this time just a quick shadow behind a house. He was carrying some kind of bag. Was the kid in there?

Carefully, quietly, Striker crawled out from under the house and began to track Wilson again. He could see the shadowy figure ahead of him, not too far away. He followed Wilson to an abandoned house and watched him go inside with the big sack.

Now it was daybreak. Striker watched the house from another crawl space, across the street from Wilson's hideout. He could hear people above, walking across the floorboards, probably getting ready to fix breakfast. Fortunately, there was no curious dog with a keen sense of smell anywhere around. A dog would have been trouble.

He thought about the bag and his next move. Darkness had been an advantage. It was still quiet. The police were apparently elsewhere, maybe rounding up search dogs. Fog rolled in. Good: this would give him some cover. He had to act. Abandoning the safety of the crawl space, he crept from bush to bush and made a low-crouched run to the abandoned house.

He listened for movement: nothing. He peered through a broken window. He saw a discarded trash bag, boxed food stacked up. He crawled under the house. There were no other sounds. He slipped around to the back of the house and onto what remained of a porch. Huddled against the house, he slowly rose to peer inside. *Elijah*. The child was sitting against a wall, tied up and gagged. He wasn't moving.

Now. There was no other choice.

The back door was unlocked. Striker stood up and opened the door swiftly, rushing to Elijah. As he reached to pick him up, Wilson stepped out of a room with a pipe. There was no time to think. Striker wrestled the pipe from Wilson's grip and struck him under the jaw. Wilson went down.

Striker untied and ungagged Elijah. Thank God, he was still breathing. Then Striker bound and tied Wilson with random items—a belt, some loose clothing, the rope Wilson had used on the boy—and dragged him to the street.

Back inside again, he scooped up Elijah and ran to the next house. There was a light on inside. He banged on the door and ran, setting the boy down on the porch. As he looked back, he saw an elderly woman open the door. She looked right at him. But then she turned to Elijah, and Striker knew the boy was safe.

Chapter 49

SLEEPY-EYED

A week later, Cameron drove to the hospital to visit John, her arm in a cast. Her injuries had left her shaken, but compared to the others, her recovery was going to be relatively swift. Alisha was still bruised up but healing, and Elijah, thank God, was uninjured and doing fine. Juan was stable, despite the blow to the head, and the doctors were amazed at his progress. But John and Sandra remained under hospital care. They were expected to fully recover, but they had both suffered severe blunt force trauma to the head.

Cameron arrived early in the morning, and John was still asleep. She sat in the corner and watched him. On his back, sleepy-eyed and foggy, he finally awoke and lay there for several long minutes.

Cameron remained silent in the chair next to the bed. His eyes fluttered a little.

After several minutes of separate solitude, Cameron ventured a soft "good morning." He turned his head toward her, smiled, and reached out his hand. She touched him and said, "Did you hear me?"

"Yes, that's nice. How are you?"

"I'm good, and you?"

"Better. I slept well. I feel good." He tried to pull a second pillow under his head to better see Cameron, but he couldn't manage it. "Well," he said, "I see I'm none the stronger!"

"The nurse tells me they're running more tests today to make sure your functions are still improving. She says you're doing great."

"Yes, I guess I'm a little off balance. They told me they sedated me for a few days, kept me unconscious, but here I am awake and looking at you. Can't beat that."

Cameron tipped her head, gazing up at him with a smile. "If you say so."

He cracked a sheepish grin.

"John, I was so worried, so scared, and now I'm just so happy to see you. I love seeing you awake. But go back to sleep. I'll be back later."

"Thanks for staying with me. I love it," he said. "How are Elijah and David?"

"Great, doing fine; everyone's fine. Sandra's improving too. She's just down the hall, doing very well. She asks about you."

"That's nice. Tell her I said hello. Hey, I can feel myself drifting off to sleep."

"Good. See you in a bit. It's been a hell of a trip, these last weeks, huh? One way to get a child's justice. But let's not do that again, okay?"

John smiled at her. "Deal," he said.

Cameron leaned down and gave him a quick kiss before saying goodbye.

It was more than two weeks before John reported back to work. He spent his time studying the numerous newspaper articles on Elijah's abduction, Sandra's encounters with Jack Wilson, and Wilson's attacks.

It was still a mystery as to who had rescued Elijah. Cameron, too, took a weeklong sabbatical to recuperate.

The entire crew welcomed John back with cards and balloons, but he had nixed a party. Once he settled into his cubicle, the head of the agency, Elizabeth, summoned both him and Cameron to the conference room.

"News outlets keep pushing for more and more information," she told them. "You've both been great at staying away from reporters, and I appreciate that. I'm not sure how long that can last, especially with this mystery person who rescued Elijah and delivered up Jack Wilson. Wilson, of course, is charged and now incommunicado." She stopped talking for a second or two, brushed her hair back from her face, let out a large breath, and relaxed back into her chair. "I'm so pleased you two are back in the office, ready to work together. We were so scared and worried. That's an understatement."

"Do you think DCF will investigate?" Cameron asked.

"Oh, that's a certainty," Elizabeth said. "We can expect plenty of hardball questions from DCF. And both of you were all over these cases, so we'll make sure you have counsel on how to handle any questions. Sound good?"

"Sounds good to me," John said.

"I wouldn't be surprised to hear some criticism," Elizabeth said. "But just remember that you were keeping Judge Crowe up to date the whole way. Because of that, she put David in shelter. You gave her an opportunity to shelter Elijah, which she rejected, but that decision ended up working out because it left Juan Martinez involved. Without him, there's no telling how badly hurt you and Alisha would have ended up being that night."

"We got lucky," Cameron said, shaking her head. "It's all just so risky. All the time."

"That's not going to end," said John.

"No shit!" Cameron said.

"You're right," John said, "and so articulate."

They laughed.

"Okay, we'll see. Come on. Let's get back to work."

Chapter 50

ONE LAST COWBOY

The next day, Cameron was back in her cubicle, scrolling through case reports. There was so much to catch up on. The receptionist called to say there was a man downstairs in cowboy boots. Charles Halstrom stood waiting in the lobby, hat in hand.

"Ms. Springer, nice to see you again. I just had to stop by and say hello." They shook hands.

"Thank you so much, Mr. Halstrom." Cameron was surprised and touched.

"Do you mind calling me Charles now?"

Cameron smiled. "Sure, Charles. How are Amy Jo and the boys?"

"They're very good, thank you, and Mary is almost back to her normal self."

"I'm so glad to hear that," Cameron said.

"I just had to thank you for sticking by my family and not giving up. I know you went out of your way with the visit to the hospital and convincing that lady lawyer to help out. I liked her a lot."

"Thank you, Charles. Do you mind if I ask John to come say hello too?"

"Fine. I'll wait here."

Cameron grabbed John, and they hurried back downstairs. John was in good shape: no bandages, no bruises, all professional looking again, with shined leather shoes.

"Mr. Halstrom, so nice to see you, especially with no alligators. Cam said you were down here."

Halstrom looked ready to herd some cows in his well-worn jeans, spurs attached to his boots, and a checkered, blue-and-white shirt. He grabbed John's hand and shook it—hard. John smiled and flinched a little.

"Sure enough, sir, I'm here. Thanks to you, Cam, and the little lady—what's her name, Lara?"

"That's right," Cameron said. "Lara Liu."

Charles took a few steps toward Cameron and John, hat in hand, and said, "I just had to say thanks. Thank you so much to both of you. All's well with us, and I hope all's well with both of you. I assume you're staying out of trouble."

Cam glanced at John. They both produced sheepish smiles.

"Yep," Cameron said. "Out of trouble, we think, or we hope." She and John laughed and thanked Halstrom for stopping by. "Don't forget to call us if we can help in any way," John said.

"Will do," he said. "Take care. I've got to head back home, repair some fences. Have to use horses to get back to that part of the ranch. That's the reason for the spurs today."

Cam and John waved goodbye. Cameron turned to John. "You know, he didn't say one thing about my broken arm. That was strange."

"Cam, honestly, I think he was probably too afraid to ask."

"Let's go to Sam's tonight. It'll be nice. I want you to go with me. Don't disappear into a corner and watch baseball. I need you."

"I'd like that," John said, reaching down to squeeze her hand. "And I need you too."

ACKNOWLEDGMENTS

I extend my appreciation to multiple friends who provided guidance and edits for this book and its earlier drafts. Special thanks go to David Kennedy and Stephanie Vulliet for their insights and edits. A thumbs-up goes to Lynn Stegner for excellent editorial assistance. Greenleaf Book Group, and its imprint River Grove Books, are much appreciated, including their editors Rebecca Logan, Anne Sanow, Hayden Seder, and Diana Coe. I am grateful for their help. Of course, any fault lines or difficulties with the story or text remain solely within my provenance and responsibility.

ABOUT THE AUTHOR

CHARLES KETCHEY JR. is a senior member of Trenam Law in Tampa, St. Petersburg, and Sarasota, Florida. Board certified by the Florida Bar in civil trial and business litigation, he specializes in corporate and bankruptcy trial and litigation. Over the course of his career, he has gained experience in child dependency cases and worked with organizations that provide assistance to families and especially to children at risk of neglect or abuse. Charlie resides in Tampa Bay with his wife, Brenda, and an extended family that includes a daughter and son and their spouses and children.